These girls are on the adventure of their lives. But with teamwork and their own special abilities, they just might be Cayenga Park's newest heroes . . .

girls
R. U. L. E.

Kayla Adams's wavy brown hair and dark, almond-shaped eyes attract attention, but her quick temper and sharp tongue keep it—especially when she stands up for her friends.

Carson McDonald has never let her hearing disability get in her way. In fact, it has forced this blonde, beautiful athlete to be extra-sensitive to her environment—qualities which make her an excellent sleuth.

Becca Fisher is a natural clown, always cracking jokes. But her sarcastic sense of humor often has a way of getting the petite, wiry girl with deep green eyes in trouble.

Sophie Schultz is intense, determined, and stubborn. Nicknamed "little bulldog" by her dad, this redhead knows what she wants and goes after it despite all obstacles, including her older brother and junior ranger, Jason!

Alex Loomis-Drake has a million facts stored in her head, and a million interests to match. But although this girl with brown, silky hair comes from a wealthy family, she isn't your usual pampered princess.

Don't miss any of the girls *R. U. L. E. adventures!*

girls R.U.L.E.

#3

SEAL ISLAND SCAM

Kris Lowe

BERKLEY JAM BOOKS, NEW YORK

GIRLS R.U.L.E.: SEAL ISLAND SCAM

A Berkley Jam Book / published by arrangement with
the author

PRINTING HISTORY
Berkley Jam edition / November 1998

The Penguin Putnam Inc. World Wide Web site address is
http://www.penguinputnam.com

ISBN: 0-425-16520-5

BERKLEY JAM BOOKS®
Berkley Jam Books are published by The Berkley Publishing Group,
a member of Penguin Putnam Inc.,
375 Hudson Street, New York, New York 10014.
BERKLEY JAM and its logo are trademarks
belonging to Berkley Publishing Corporation.

PRINTED IN THE UNITED STATES OF AMERICA

10   9   8   7   6   5   4   3   2   1

For Fiona, as always.
Thank you for teaching me about seals and sea lions.

girls R.U.L.E.

#3

SEAL ISLAND SCAM

KAYLA

ONE

I picked up the whistle that was hanging around my neck and blew it hard. "Hey, you out there! No diving from the float!" I called, cupping my hand to my mouth. I sighed. "Like I haven't told those same kids that about a million times today already."

Becca Fisher, who was sitting on the lifeguard stand beside me, snickered. "Maybe their brains got water-logged from all that swimming," she joked.

I managed to smile. But the truth was I was feeling kind of stressed. The kiddie beach was really crowded today, way more crowded than I'd seen it in the last several weeks since I'd started working as a Cayenga Park junior ranger. Becca and I, along with the other junior rangers, take turns doing different jobs in the park. Lifeguarding at the kiddie beach is usually a fun assignment. But today it looked as if practically every little kid in the whole town of Cayenga had decided to come to the park beach. Even with Becca there to share the job, it felt like an awful lot of responsibility to watch out for everyone's safety.

Becca took off her green Cayenga Park baseball cap and fanned herself with it. "Wow, this sun is starting to make me feel like a broiled Becca-burger," she said. "We never had fall days this hot back in New York."

"This is pretty hot for California, too," I assured her. "I mean, November's usually warm, but not this warm."

"I guess this is Indian summer, then," Becca commented.

"Actually, Becca," I said carefully, "that might not be the greatest way to put it."

"What do you mean, Kayla?" Becca looked confused.

"Well, if you think about it, there's nothing 'Indian' about warm weather late in the year. And some people even say the expression came about because European settlers back in the eighteen hundreds thought that the

4

extra weeks of warm weather would give the Native Americans more of a chance to attack their settlements."

"Oh, wow, I had no idea it meant anything like that," Becca said. She grinned. "From now on I'll just call it 'disgustingly hot fall weather,' I promise."

I grinned back, glad I had said something to Becca. I guess I'm kind of extra aware of that kind of thing because I'm part Native American myself. Actually, my heritage is a combination of Native American, African-American, Mexican-American, and Chinese-American. But the way I see it, it doesn't matter what your background is. You don't have to be a member of a certain group to care whether or not you might be offending someone.

Just then Becca nudged me with her elbow. "Hey, look out there." She pointed out toward the horizon. "In the sky."

I gazed toward where she was pointing. Beyond the buoys that marked off the swimming area, several Jet Skis crisscrossed the water, spraying foam. In the distance I could see two fishing boats and the three small islands that people in Cayenga call "the Three Sisters": Surf Island, Gull Island, and Seal Island. Low in the sky above them I spotted a parasailor suspended by a parachute tethered to the back of a boat.

"That looks so cool," Becca said with admiration in her voice. "I'd love to try parasailing sometime."

That's one of the things I like about Becca. She's totally enthusiastic, and she's open to just about anything. We're pretty different that way. I'm definitely more the type to look before I leap. But that's one of the cool things about the five girls in the Ranger Unit Learning Extension—or Girls R.U.L.E.—as we're called. Becca, Carson, Alex, Sophie, and I are all really different, and each one of us has something unique to bring to rangering.

Just then I heard a high-pitched squeal from below the lifeguard stand to my left. Concerned, I turned to look. A girl who seemed about my age, around fourteen or fifteen, was chasing a bottomless toddler around a large beach blanket with a diaper in her hand. The toddler seemed to think the whole thing was a big joke. He was laughing and screaming as he ran. Meanwhile, twin boys who looked about five years old were sitting on the beach blanket, fighting over a half-inflated inner tube. Nearby a slightly younger girl in a floppy sun hat was tossing small rocks into the air.

"Is that one girl really supposed to be taking care of all four of those kids by herself?" I wondered out loud. The baby-sitter had gotten hold of the toddler and was struggling to get the diaper on him now. The twins were yelling at each other. The young girl in the sand stood up, her hands full of rocks.

"If so, then her job makes ours look easy," Becca commented.

A seagull landed beside the girl with the floppy hat. She threw a rock at it.

"Hey, little girl!" I called to her.

But she either hadn't heard me or was ignoring me. She lobbed another rock. The seagull fluttered into the air and then landed again beside her.

"Hey, there!" I called out again. But she kept at it. I can't stand it when people are cruel to animals. The way I see it, all of nature's creatures have a right to be treated with respect and kindness. *Besides,* I thought, *throwing rocks on the beach is definitely dangerous, no matter how you look at it. Another kid could end up getting hit.* I turned to Becca. "Where'd that girl who's supposed to be taking care of them go?"

"Looks like she's just starting the second lap of the

race," Becca replied, pointing toward the other end of the beach.

The teenage girl was running after the twins now, with the toddler on her hip and a bottle of suntan lotion in her hand. Back at the blanket the girl in the floppy hat was still throwing rocks. I decided I had to do something.

"I'll be right back," I told Becca. I climbed down from the lifeguard stand and walked across the hot sand toward the little girl.

"Hi," I said, squatting down beside her.

"Hi," she answered, squinting at me in the sunlight.

I pointed to the rocks in her hand. "Those are some pretty cool rocks you have there," I told her. "Cool enough to start a collection with. I don't think it's such a good idea to use them as weapons, though."

She stared at me a moment and then glanced toward the seagull pecking the sand nearby.

"It's just a dumb bird," she said.

"That's not just any ordinary bird," I said to her. "Don't you know who that is?"

She shook her head.

"That's Clarence. Clarence has lived on this beach

since he was just a little chick. He's got a wife somewhere near here named Mabel."

It was easy to make up the story as I went along. I used to do that kind of thing all the time when I was a kid. My mom says that when I was four I named all of the tomatoes in our garden. I was convinced that they were all part of a big family, and I wouldn't let my mom pick them. My parents always tease me about how we didn't get to eat any of our tomatoes that year.

"Clarence and Mabel have three little chicks," I continued. "Rufus, Gertie, and Chee. Chee's feeling really hungry right now, but Rufus and Gertie are saying, 'Don't worry, Mommy and Daddy went to get us some nice fish for lunch. They'll be back soon.'"

The girl was smiling now. "Is Chee a boy or a girl?" she asked.

"A girl," I answered. I paused. "Now, you wouldn't want anything to happen to Chee's daddy while he's supposed to be out looking for fish for her, would you? You wouldn't want Clarence to accidentally get hit by a rock or something."

The girl's big brown eyes grew serious. She shook her head.

"I had a feeling you'd see it that way," I said. "And

you be careful of the other seagulls, too. You never know which ones might be one of Chee's aunts or grandfathers or cousins."

The little girl nodded solemnly.

I'm glad I climbed down from the lifeguard stand to talk to her instead of just yelling at her, I decided. All she needed was a little help looking at the situation from the seagull's point of view.

Just then I heard a voice behind me. "Is everything okay?"

I turned and saw the teenage baby-sitter standing in the sand. The toddler was still in her arms, and she was holding one of the twins by the hand. The other twin was nowhere in sight.

"Erica, you weren't up to trouble again, were you?" the baby-sitter asked, sounding worried.

"Everything's fine," I assured her. I gave the girl in the floppy hat a quick wink. "We were just talking."

"Good," the girl answered, hitching the baby up in her arm.

"Tracy, I'm hot," the little boy holding her hand complained. "I want to go in the water."

"In a minute," the girl answered, an edge of exasperation in her voice.

"Are you taking care of all these kids by yourself?" I asked Tracy.

She nodded. "That's right." She sighed. "Every Saturday from nine to three. Mr. and Mrs. Warren like me to take them out of the house."

"Tracy," the little boy whined again. "I'm hot! Jeff's in the water. Can't I go in, too?"

"In a minute," Tracy said sharply. "Besides, Jeff's not in the water. He's playing in the sand." She turned to me. "I tried to tell the Warrens I could use some help with the kids, but they never seem to get around to hiring another baby-sitter."

The little boy tugged on Tracy's T-shirt. "Jeff is too in the water!" he insisted. "He took the tube and he went in. It's not fair! It's my turn to use the tube!"

An expression of alarm crossed Tracy's face. She turned to the little boy. "Jack, Jeff didn't really go in swimming without me, did he?"

Suddenly I heard a sharp whistle. I turned to face the lifeguard stand. Becca was on her feet and about to jump down into the sand. She saw me and pointed toward the water.

I quickly scanned the ocean. There, beyond the children playing near the shore and beyond the swimmers, beyond the raft, even, I could make out a tiny head bobbing on top of the waves.

"Oh, no! It's Jeff!" Tracy cried beside me. "He can't swim!"

I didn't hesitate another moment. As fast as I could I took off across the hot sand and headed for the ocean. I already had a head start, and I knew I could get there before Becca. The waves were cold against my hot legs as I charged into the water, but I hardly noticed. As soon as I'd cleared the breakers, I dived in and swam straight out from the shore.

After a few dozen strokes I paused to get my bearings, treading water and gulping air. The sun was glaring, but I could just make out Jeff in the distance, his tiny face barely visible above the inner tube. I took a deep breath and swam toward him, trying to keep my strokes even and fast.

A few minutes later I stopped again, expecting to find myself right beside him. But the little boy was still not nearly within my reach. In fact, I had only made a little progress in shortening the distance between us.

The current is taking him farther out, I realized suddenly. *In just a few moments he'll be past the buoys that separate the swimming area from the water-sports area and the ocean beyond.*

I knew I had to get to him quickly. I dived back into the water and swam as hard and as fast as I could, only turning my head to breathe every three or four strokes. My shoulders were aching, and my lungs felt as if they were about to burst, but I concentrated on slicing my arms into the water and kicking my feet.

When I surfaced again, Jeff was only a few yards away, crying and clutching his inner tube as the choppy waves bounced him along.

"Don't worry, Jeff!" I called to him. "I'm coming to help you. You just hang on."

A few quick strokes later I was beside him. He reached out, sobbing, and clung to me. His grip was incredibly tight, and I could see by his face that he was terrified.

"I'm sorry," he wailed. "I didn't mean to. I only wanted to try out the new tube."

"It's okay, Jeff," I said, trying to soothe him as I treaded water. "I'm going to get you back to shore."

But I could see that the current had already carried us out even farther. The beach looked about a million miles away. *I'd better get moving before it's too late,* I realized.

I decided it would probably be best to keep Jeff in the tube and to use it as a flotation aid. The way he was clinging to me, it was going to be a difficult enough rescue, and I could use all the help I could get.

I managed to rearrange our bodies so that his chin was cradled in the crook of my elbow—the rescue position we'd been taught in the water-safety course all the junior rangers had to take—and started paddling hard back toward shore with my free hand. It was slow going, but we were definitely making progress. Soon the buoys that marked the swimming zone were right in front of me.

Just then I heard a tremendous roar to my left. I turned my head in surprise, just as a bright blue Jet Ski sped by—barely missing us.

"Hey!" I yelled as a huge spray of water from the Jet Ski hit me in the face. "Watch out!"

That was way too close, I said to myself. *We could have had our heads taken off!* I looked around. We were practically inside the swim zone. *They definitely shouldn't be driving those things so close to the buoys,* I thought angrily.

I noticed that Jeff was shivering in my grip. Whether it was from fear or cold I didn't know. One thing I did know was that I had to get him back to shore as soon as I could.

I continued to paddle. A crowd had gathered on the beach to watch the rescue. Becca was on her feet on the lifeguard stand, shading her eyes as she monitored our progress.

Slowly and steadily I managed to tow Jeff and the tube back toward shore. My arm was aching from paddling against the current, but I tried not to think about it. I kept my goal—the beach—in my mind and in my sight. *Don't give up until you reach it,* I told myself. *Keep going. Concentrate.*

Finally my foot scraped against the sandy bottom. *We made it!* I let out a huge sigh of relief. On the shore I could see Tracy anxiously pacing back and forth, the baby in her arms and a terrified expression on her face.

As I pulled Jeff out of the shallow water and onto the sand, Tracy ran to him. She threw her arms around him and began scolding him all at once.

"Jeff! I told you never to go in the water without me!" she cried. She shook her head. "Oh, thank goodness you're okay!" Then she turned to me. "Thank you so much! I'm so sorry. I left him playing by the shore, and he knew he wasn't supposed to go in."

I was breathing so heavily I could barely answer. I bent down to rest my hands on my knees, the water dripping off my shoulders into the sand.

"I really appreciate what you did," Tracy said to me. "If there's anything I can do to thank you . . ."

"As a matter of fact," I said, between breaths, "there is something you can do." I looked at her. "When you bring the kids back home this afternoon, tell the Warrens they've got to get a second sitter right away. Tell them you're quitting unless they do."

Tracy nodded silently. I could tell she felt bad.

Just then someone threw a towel around my shoulders. I turned and saw Becca standing behind me in the sand.

"Nice work," she said, nodding at me with a serious expression on her face. "That's two rescues for you today, Kayla."

"Two?" I repeated, standing up and smoothing my wet hair back.

"Sure." She grinned. "First the bird, and then the boy."

16

I managed to smile back, and even let out a little laugh. But as I looked down at my knees, I suddenly noticed that they were shaking. In fact, they were shaking so hard I wondered if they would ever stop.

TWO

"Eeeeeow!" I forced the sound out of my gut and up through my throat. *"Eeeeeow!"* I did it again. It felt great.

I stared at an imaginary spot in front of me as I ran through the kata, which is a series of steps, punches, and kicks. In karate, kata are like routines: you go through them to practice your form and give yourself a sense of balance and power. To me they're always really calming.

In fact, standing in my spot in the front row of students, moving slowly together from one position to the next, I felt a sense of relief for the first time since I'd pulled little Jeff Warren out of the water earlier that day. I hadn't realized how tense I'd been—or how afraid. It was as if I had pushed all the fear deep down inside me and somehow managed to leave it behind so I could get the job done.

But now, looking back, I realized I'd been in a really dangerous situation. I'd been so concerned about getting Jeff to safety that I hadn't really considered the fact that I might get swept away by the current as well.

Not to mention that stupid Jet Ski, I added to myself. *It's bad enough that everyone has to listen to those loud motors roaring all day on the beach without having to worry that they're going to drive by the swimming zone and run people over.* I decided to say something about it to Ranger Abe Mayfield, the head ranger at Cayenga Park, at our next junior ranger meeting. Maybe he'd agree to have the Jet Ski people use an area that wasn't so close to the swimmers.

Suddenly, just as we were getting to the end of the last kata, the students on either side of me broke away from what they were doing and stood at attention, their bodies rigid. Glancing around, I realized that my dad had come into the room. I joined the rest of the class in a deep bow from the waist. My father solemnly returned the bow. Don't get me wrong, my dad's not a strict, formal person or anything. Outside the class-room he's totally easygoing and friendly. But it's a karate tradition that everyone's supposed to stop what they're doing and bow respectfully when the head *sensei,* or teacher, appears—even if he does happen to be your dad.

I'm pretty used to all that stuff, though. My dad has owned the Golden Path Martial Arts Center since I was two years old, and I've been studying karate there since I was five. I'm a purple belt now, which is the fourth belt up in our type of karate.

My father nodded to Sensei Tada, the instructor for our class, and she gave us the signal to start the final kata again. I could feel my father's eyes on me as I carefully went through the routine. It's true that my dad is a really sweet guy, but he's also always been my toughest critic, at least where karate is concerned. I totally appreciate it, though. I know it's thanks to a combination of my dad's attention and my own hard work that I've made it to purple belt.

We finished the kata and bowed to Sensei Tada. She returned the bow and dismissed the class.

Once we were outside the classroom, my father put his arm around my shoulders. "Nice form today," he complimented me. "You seemed a little unsteady, though. Is anything bothering you?"

I smiled and let out a deep breath. My dad's always been pretty good at reading my emotions. "I guess I'm still a little shaky," I told him. "I had to do a water rescue at the beach today, and I'm only just now realizing how scary the whole thing was."

My father looked concerned. "What happened?"

I quickly explained about Jeff and the tube and the current. When I finished, my father nodded slowly. "I'm proud of you, Kayla. You did the right thing," he said. Then he pursed his lips. "Although I can't say the idea of you out there in the current doesn't worry me."

"Me, too, Dad," I told him. "I don't even think I realized how terrified I was until it was over." I lowered my voice. "The truth is I don't know if I'd be able to do it again."

"You'll come through if someone needs you, Kayla," my father said. "I'm sure of it." He patted me on the shoulder. "Now, why don't you go get changed while I close up shop around here? Your mother will be stopping by in a few minutes to pick us up. I thought we'd all go out and try that new Pakistani restaurant on Ortega Drive."

As I headed down the hall, I couldn't help wishing I

had the same confidence in myself that my father seemed to have in me. I remembered what it was like trying to swim against the current and get back to shore, with the people on the beach looking so far away. *Would I be able to do it again if I had to?* I wondered. I couldn't be sure.

As I rounded the corner toward the locker rooms, my eye was caught by a framed quotation hanging on one of the walls. My mom has made a few of these up for my dad with various quotes that he likes on them, and they decorate the walls of the dojo, or karate school. This one was written in my mom's familiar calligraphy on deep purple paper.

DISLIKE EVIL,

FEEL PEACE,

TAKE PLEASURE IN

LEARNING . . .

AND FEAR WILL

DISAPPEAR.

—BUDDHA

Buddha was this ancient deep-thinker guy from India. A lot of my dad's quotes are from him. Some of the stuff he says is really cool—like "No one on earth is more deserving of your love and affection than yourself." I really think that's true. If you can't love yourself, then forget about really loving anyone else.

But this time Buddha definitely wasn't doing much for me on this fear thing. Somehow I had the feeling that Buddha hadn't ever been a lifeguard at the Cayenga Park kiddie beach.

THREE

The following Saturday morning I rode my bike through the park's north entrance, waved to the ranger on duty at the entrance booth, and coasted down the hill to the park headquarters building. Every Saturday there's a big meeting at the park for all the junior rangers, girls and boys. Ranger Abe likes to update us on whatever's going on in the park and to talk to us about the coming week.

It was a sunny morning, but the air was nowhere near as hot as it had been the week before, which was a relief. I parked my bike in the bike rack at the side of the building and walked inside. Ranger Abe hadn't arrived yet, but there was already a big crowd of kids in the main meeting room, mostly guys as usual. The boys' division of the junior rangers is much bigger than the girls'. That's because their division has been around for ten years, so lots of guys have had a chance to try out. The girls' division only had its first tryouts this year. Five of us passed the qualifying test, so for now, at least, we're the whole division.

I think it's totally despicable that the boys' division was around for that long before anyone ever even thought of the idea of letting girls try out. I just can't stand that kind of totally obvious unfairness.

But at least we've got a girls' division now, I reminded myself. *And we're proving that we can do at least as good a job as the guys—if not better.*

I spotted Becca, along with Carson McDonald, another junior ranger, sitting together on the far side of the room. I started to approach them, and Carson looked up immediately and waved to me. Sometimes I really think that Carson has some kind of ESP or something. She almost seems as if she knows what's going to happen even before it does.

Carson says it's just that she's trained herself to notice things that other people miss. She says she has to be that way, to make up for her disability. You see,

Carson has only partial hearing in one ear, and none at all in the other. The way she explains it, she's had to teach herself to be really aware with all her other senses to make up for what she doesn't hear.

I pulled up a chair and sat beside them. "Hey, guys, what's new?" I greeted them, taking care as always to let Carson see my face so she could read my lips.

"What's new, huh?" Becca grinned and ran her hand through her short brown hair. "Batter-fried eel, that's what."

I looked at her quizzically.

"It's the latest dish on the menu down at the Cayenga Grill," Becca explained. "We've got this section on the menu board called 'What's New,' and I just added batter-fried eel to it yesterday. When you said that, it reminded me."

"Oh," I said. Becca's mom and stepdad own a restaurant in town, and she helps out there sometimes. Barry, Becca's stepfather, is a really adventurous cook. He's always trying out wild new recipes.

Carson screwed up her face. "Batter-fried eel? As in an actual eel? Is that good?"

"Totally incredible," Becca assured her. "At least the way Barry makes it. There's some new fishing

27

operation down by the docks that's selling all this fresh exotic seafood—eel, octopus, stuff like that. Barry's having the time of his life. You guys should stop by and try some of the new seafood dishes."

"Actually, I think I'll pass," I said. I'm a vegetarian. I don't eat meat, chicken, or fish.

"Oh, right," Becca said. "I forgot. Sorry." Then she brightened. "Hey, who knows? Maybe Barry'll come up with something you can eat, like Seaweed Surprise."

I laughed. "The seaweed part sounds okay to me," I replied. "My mom gets dried seaweed from the health-food store and puts it in soups and salads sometimes. It's the 'surprise' part I'd be worried about."

Carson shook her head, and her blonde ponytail swung back and forth. "Eels and seaweed? You guys make me feel like my family eats the most boring stuff in the whole world. At my house we think it's a pretty big deal just to put croutons in the salad!"

We all laughed.

Just then Sophie Schultz, another member of the girls' division, walked into the room. She had on her usual funky clothes—ripped, patched cutoff jeans and a flowy peasant blouse—and she still wore a cast on her right arm from an accident she'd had a while back on a horse. With her was her brother, Jason.

"Wow, look," Becca said, looking surprised. "Do you think Sophie and Jason called a truce?"

I had to admit, like Becca, I was pretty startled to see Sophie and her brother arrive at the meeting together. Jason's a junior ranger, too, but he and Sophie don't exactly get along. If you ask me, it's pretty much Jason's doing. He seems to like to give Sophie a hard time whenever he can.

"Hey, Schultz, over here!" a loud voice boomed from across the room. It was Rick Neely, the unofficial head of the boys' division, and Jason's best friend.

Rick and Jason high-fived in the center of the room. Sophie rolled her eyes and continued walking toward us. She plopped down on an empty folding chair beside Becca with a loud sigh.

"Remind me never to agree to ride here with Jason again," she said in an exasperated voice. "Or any-where, for that matter. My mom had to work at the hospital today, so she offered to drop us off on her way. But all we did was argue—about who was sitting where, what music we were going to listen to . . . we even argued about my hat!"

"Your hat?" I asked incredulously. Being an only child, I have to say I'm sometimes amazed at the stuff sisters and brothers fight about.

"What was the deal with your hat?" Carson wanted to know.

A grin spread across Sophie's face. She reached into the back pocket of her shorts, pulled out her green Cayenga Park baseball cap, and plopped it on top of her long red curls. At least, I was pretty sure it was her Cayenga Park baseball cap. It was kind of hard to tell, since it was just about completely covered in "GIRLS R.U.L.E." patches.

"I have to admit, I did it just to annoy Jason and Rick anyway," Sophie whispered, her eyes twinkling mischievously.

I laughed. "Sophie, is *that* why you asked me for extra patches last week?"

The patches are something special my mom designed for us. A little while after the girls' division was first formed, I realized that the initials of the official name for the group—"Ranger Unit Learning Extension"—spelled "R.U.L.E." I figured that meant our division could be "GIRLS R.U.L.E." The others agreed that it was a cool name, and Ranger Abe said it was fine with him, so I asked my mom, who's an artist, to design some patches for us. Ever since then, we'd all worn "GIRLS R.U.L.E." patches on our Cayenga Park hats, T-shirts, and windbreakers. Nobody had gone quite so far with it as Sophie, though.

Just then Ranger Abe walked in, and the room grew silent. We all waited as he made his way to the front of the room.

Sophie leaned toward me. "Hey, where's Alex?" she whispered.

I shrugged. "It's not like her to be late for a meeting." Alex Loomis-Drake is the fifth member of GIRLS R.U.L.E. Alex lives on the other side of the park, in Cayenga Heights, but she and I go to school together, at Harmon Academy. Sophie, Carson, and Becca go to a different school, Cayenga High. "I'm sure she'll be here," I reassured Sophie.

Ranger Abe cleared his throat. "Well, junior rangers, it was another successful week in the park, thanks in part to all of you. We had a record number of visitors turn out for this time of year, due to the unusually warm weather last weekend. But you all pitched in and handled the situation well."

"You can count on us to save the day, Ranger Abe!"

Rick Neely called out boastfully from his seat on the other side of the room.

"Actually, speaking of saving the day," Ranger Abe said, "I'd like to take this opportunity to thank one of our members for a heroic act last weekend." He smiled at me. "Kayla Adams performed a water rescue of a young boy. Kayla, well done."

"Thanks, Ranger Abe," I said, feeling a flush of pride at his words.

"Thank *you*," Ranger Abe replied. "It's quick thinking and fast action like that that keeps the park safe for visitors."

That reminded me of something. I raised my hand.

Ranger Abe nodded toward me. "Yes, Kayla? Did you want to say something?"

"Well, speaking of keeping the park safe for visitors, I think there may be a dangerous situation involving the Jet Skis near the kiddie beach," I said.

Ranger Abe looked concerned. "Are they crossing into the swimming area?" he asked quickly.

"Not exactly," I replied. "But they're coming awfully close. I really think it would be a good idea for the park to move the water-sports area farther offshore."

"I agree with you a hundred percent," Ranger Abe

replied. "Unfortunately, that's not our decision to make. Only the swimming area is within park jurisdiction. We have no say over what happens beyond the buoys in that particular area." He sighed. "And frankly, it's only gotten worse over the past few years. It used to be you'd get a water-skier crossing too close now and then. But ever since that Jet Ski rental operation opened in town last year, it's like a superhighway out there. It's not safe for swimmers or for marine life, either. However, I'm sorry, Kayla. There's nothing we can do about it."

There's nothing we can do—those must be my five least-favorite words in the English language, I thought with frustration. *There must be some way to keep those people on Jet Skis farther from the beach. But how?*

Ranger Abe turned to the clipboard in his hand. "All right then, let's get on to the business of the coming week and hand out the job assignments for today so we can get you all out into the park as soon as possible. . . ."

Just then the door opened, and Alex walked in, her pale skin looking flushed under her dark hair.

"Sorry I'm late," she said breathlessly, grabbing a chair near the back.

"That's all right, Alex," Ranger Abe replied. "I was just about to give out the day's assignments."

Ranger Abe proceeded to go through the roster of jobs, assigning them to various junior rangers. I hadn't had to lifeguard again during the past week, and I have to admit I was a little worried that Ranger Abe might assign me to the kiddie beach again, as he had the Saturday before. *You'll do fine,* I tried to tell myself. *You're a strong swimmer, and you love the water. Besides, what are the chances you'll have to do another rescue like that one?*

I tried to shake off the queasy feeling in my stomach. *After all,* I reasoned, *I'm going to have to lifeguard again eventually, even if it's not today. I'd better get used to the idea.*

But I have to admit I felt relieved when Ranger Abe assigned me to the coastal patrol job and gave me Alex as my partner. I'd never done coastal patrol before, but I knew it basically consisted of checking out the beaches and other park coastal areas by boat.

I was pretty sure that I could handle that. It wasn't likely that I was going to have to rescue anyone.

FOUR

Twenty minutes later Alex and I sat in a small green Cayenga Park boat, bouncing along as we headed away from shore. The wind in my hair and the ocean mist on my face felt great, and I closed my eyes, feeling the rhythm of the boat as it skimmed over the waves.

"This is great," Alex said from her spot behind me.

I took a deep breath. "Mmmmm, isn't it?" I said. I turned to look at her. But instead of enjoying the surroundings, Alex was bent over the outboard motor, studying it intently.

"Yeah, it's got this incredible easy-start ignition," she said, still examining the motor. "Just the touch of a button and it starts up. Not like those older models with the cord you have to pull. It's really a much better design."

I had to laugh. "Alex, only you would find beauty in a greasy old motor instead of noticing the scenery," I said.

"Hey," Alex said, "don't forget that it's this little beauty right here that makes it possible for us to be out here enjoying the scenery in the first place." She patted the side of the motor.

I laughed again. "Good point." I twisted in my seat to face her and tightened the strap on my orange life preserver. "So, you've done this coastal patrol thing before, right? What exactly are we supposed to be looking for out here anyway?" I asked. "Wrecked ships? Bottles with messages in them? Undiscovered islands?" I laughed.

Alex laughed, too. "Actually, I think it's more like people swimming in unauthorized areas and boaters dumping garbage," she replied. "Nothing too exciting. But if you're in the mood for undiscovered islands, I can show you something pretty cool."

"Oh, yeah?" I said curiously.

Alex nodded. Wordlessly she turned the boat, and we veered off to the southwest, picking up speed. As we headed farther out to sea, the wind became stronger.

"Where are we going?" I called to Alex.

She yelled something back to me, but the wind was blowing in the wrong direction, and I couldn't catch it. I waited and looked around.

I soon realized that we were headed toward the Three Sisters—Surf Island, Gull Island, and Seal Island. *Is this really what Alex means by "undiscovered islands"?* I wondered, surprised. *Everybody in Cayenga knows about these islands! They're visible from practically anywhere on shore.* All my life I'd looked out at the water and seen those solid, unchanging three masses of rock in the ocean against the horizon, and I was sure Alex had, too. What was so undiscovered about this?

It soon became clear that Alex was headed toward the largest of the three, Seal Island. I'd never been this close to the island before, and I was a little surprised at how large it actually was. As I stared at it, something suddenly caught my eye. Something that looked as if it was moving. I squinted and stared harder. Suddenly I realized that the whole surface of the island was in motion. The dark, lumpy shapes that I had assumed were rock were actually *alive.*

Seals! I thought excitedly, realizing what I was seeing. *The whole island is covered with seals!* I leaned forward in the boat to get a better look.

As we drew closer to the island, I made out seals of varying sizes, glistening and dark as they sunbathed on the rocks. In the water nearby, several others dived and swam about playfully. I stared, amazed.

Alex cut the motor and the boat slowed. Now that it was quiet, I could hear the seals barking.

"I can't believe this!" I said, turning to face Alex. "I've seen this island in the distance for years, and I never knew there were seals here." I grinned. "Of course, I guess I should have thought of it. After all, it *is* called Seal Island."

"It's a pretty cool place, isn't it?" Alex said. "I first came out here when I was a little kid. Some friends of my parents' took us out here on their yacht. There were actually a lot less seals here then. More room for people. I remember we even had a picnic on the island."

I gazed out at the island. *It's hard to imagine there ever being room there for human beings to stand, let alone have a picnic,* I thought. *I guess the seal population has really grown a lot since back then.* I looked around. A few of the seals were quite a bit smaller than the rest, and I realized they were probably babies, or youngsters, *I suppose this is a pretty good place to raise a family, if you're a seal.*

We sat there for about ten minutes as the seals swam, played, and warmed themselves in the sun. Watching them, I felt as if I could stay there forever. But when Alex started up the motor again and turned the boat away from the island, I didn't say anything. I knew we had to get back to our patrol. But I also knew I was going to come back to Seal Island again the first chance I got.

FIVE

"They were *so* amazing," I said for about the tenth time. "You guys should really go see them."

"They sound cute," Sophie said. "Especially the babies."

I shook my head. "I just can't believe they've been out there all this time, and I never saw them before."

It was later that same afternoon, and Alex and I had met up with Sophie, Becca, and Carson back at park headquarters. I was telling them all about the seals. In fact, the seals had pretty much been the only thing on my mind all afternoon.

"I've always known they were out there, but I never actually went to see them," Carson said. "My mom told me about them." Carson's mother is a Cayenga Park ranger. In fact, Carson practically grew up in the park. She knows more about it than any of us.

"Is Seal Island actually part of the park?" I asked Carson.

"I think it technically belongs to the town," Carson answered. "But from what my mom says, the town kind of handed over that little patch of ocean to the rangers to oversee long ago."

"Too bad the town didn't do that with the water-sports area near the kiddie beach," I said unhappily.

"You're really upset about this Jet Ski thing, aren't you, Kayla?" Alex asked with concern.

"Well, she *was* almost made into a pancake by one last weekend," Becca pointed out. "I saw the whole thing. It was definitely pretty scary."

"I bet," Sophie said sympathetically.

"It just really frustrates me when people act irresponsible and inconsiderate like that," I said.

"Uh-oh," Becca said. "Watch out, everyone. Super-Kayla's on another mission. Last weekend it was seagull safety, and now it's Jet Ski justice!"

I managed to laugh. But I was still upset. Then I thought of something. "Hey, Becca, that gives me an idea."

"What?" Becca asked.

"What you said, about the seagulls and the Jet Skis," I replied.

"Let me guess," Becca said. "You want to get the seagulls to drive Jet Skis? Or, I know, maybe you want to see if you can get that little girl on the beach to throw her rocks at the Jet Skis, instead of the seagulls!"

"No, no," I said quickly. "But maybe there is a connection between the two. Listen. The way I finally got that little girl to stop throwing rocks at the seagulls was to reason with her. All I did was explain to her why what she was doing was wrong, and help her see things from another point of view."

"So that's what you want to do with the Jet Ski drivers?" Carson asked doubtfully.

"Not the drivers," I said. "That would be impossible. There are probably way too many different people who go out and rent those things each day. But maybe I can talk to whoever runs the Jet Ski rental place."

"I think it sounds like a great idea," Sophie said enthusiastically.

"Sure, go for it," Alex agreed. "I mean, it's worth a try."

"Sounds like a plan to me," Becca said. "I'll even go with you if you want, Kayla."

A little while later Becca and I walked down Main Street toward Ocean View Road, which runs by the town marina. We made a right at the water and walked along the docks in the direction of the yacht club.

"Hey, look!" Becca said, pointing. "Conti's Catch! That's the new place where Barry's been getting his weird fish."

A wide wooden stand sat at the edge of the dock with a sign above it. Behind the stand a large fishing boat was docked. As we got closer I could see the multicolored fish displayed in heaps on the stand.

"Wow, look at all these," Becca said. "There are types of fish here I've never even seen before. Look at those orange ones. I wonder what they are."

I turned away a little. The truth was, the sight of all those dead fish, their mouths gaping and their black eyes staring, made me feel a little sick.

A man in rubber fisherman's overalls and boots waved to us from the deck of the boat. "Be with you in a minute."

"That's okay," Becca answered. "We're not buying. Just looking."

The man chuckled. "More spectators, huh? I'm starting to think I should charge admission."

"Well, you do have some pretty unusual-looking fish here," Becca pointed out.

"Yeah, well, Carl Conti knows where to go looking for them," the man said with obvious pride. "I got my special techniques, too."

Special techniques, huh? I hope he's not going to tell us all about those, I thought, my stomach getting queasier by the minute.

Just then Mr. Conti picked up a large black bucket. From the way he moved, I could tell that it was pretty full, and heavy, too. He bent over a red plastic bucket on the deck and began pouring some of the contents of the black bucket into it.

When I saw what was coming out of that bucket I gasped in disgust. Whatever it was, it was awful. It looked like blood and guts and pieces of meat.

"What is that?" I asked in horror.

Mr. Conti grinned. "I'm afraid I can't tell you that. Company secret. It's my special bait."

"That stuff is disgusting," Becca said, screwing up her face.

I couldn't have agreed more. I'd definitely had enough. "Can we get out of here now, Becca?" I said urgently.

"Sure," she answered. "Let's go." She waved to Mr. Conti. "Catch you later! Get it? Catch?" She laughed. She turned to me as we walked away. "I wonder what that stuff in the bucket was."

"I don't think I want to know," I said, trying to get the image of the red-streaked slop out of my mind.

We turned a corner, and suddenly a large blue-and-white sign appeared in front of us:

SALTY DOG WATER SPORTS
STRAIGHT AHEAD
RENTALS & SALES
WATER SKIS   KAYAKS
WINDSURFERS   JET SKIS

"I guess that must be it," I said, continuing in the direction of the sign.

A few minutes later another blue-and-white sign appeared.

```
YOU ARE GETTING CLOSER!
SALTY DOG AWAITS YOU!
```

And a few minutes after that:

```
YOU'RE ALMOST THERE!
FUN IN THE SUN IS JUST AROUND
THE CORNER!
```

"These signs are so ridiculous," I commented.

"They must have gone up pretty recently," Becca commented. "I was just down here a month or so ago, and they definitely weren't around then. I would have noticed them."

"How could anyone *not* notice them?" I asked. "They're so big and obnoxious." I sighed. "But I guess that's the whole point—to attract attention."

"And it looks like it's working," Becca said, pointing.

Up ahead of us was a blue-and-white building with the words SALTY DOG painted onto its roof in white. Standing outside the building was a small crowd of people who appeared to be waiting to get in.

"Wow, I had no idea this place was so popular," I said in disbelief.

"Yeah, maybe my mom and Barry should get a bunch of those signs for the restaurant," Becca commented with a little laugh.

I walked up to a tall woman who was dressed in a bathing suit and shorts.

"Excuse me," I said. "Is this the line to get in?"

She shook her head. "There is no line to get in. We're waiting for them to open."

I stared at her in surprise. "They're closed? But it's the middle of the afternoon."

"Don't I know it," the woman replied. "I've been waiting here for over an hour. Nobody knows where they are."

Just then I heard the loud roar of an engine. A bright blue convertible sports car drove up and came to a stop with a screech in front of the crowd. Sitting in the car were a man and woman who looked as if they were in their twenties. Both had jet-black hair and turned-up noses. Even though they both wore dark sunglasses, it was clear right away that they were brother and sister, possibly even twins.

The young man and woman sprang from the car and pushed their way through the crowd to the small building.

"All right, everyone!" the man announced. "We're here now. You can all come inside."

"We've been waiting out here forever to get our rental deposits back!" someone in the crowd complained. "Where've you been?"

The woman shot a nasty look in the direction of the complaint. "It just so happens that my brother and I had some important business to take care of, if you must know," she replied. "But we're open now, so come on in if you want."

"Wow, it's hard to imagine how they manage to keep their customers with that kind of attitude," I said in a low voice to Becca as we joined the group making its way toward the building.

Becca nodded. "I know. Still, they must be doing something right. Look at all these people."

Yeah, look at all these people who just spent the day crowding up that water-sports area near the kiddie beach, I thought with frustration.

We followed the crowd inside to a large open room with exposed beams and a slanted ceiling. Water-sports gear and equipment hung from hooks on every available surface. There was everything from surfboards and windsurfer sails to wet suits and sunglasses. The man and woman from the car stood behind a broad counter, and a wrinkled tan pug ran around the room sniffing at people's heels. Through some windows behind the counter I could make out an outdoor area full of Jet Skis, windsurfers, and other equipment.

After a few minutes the crowd had cleared out. Becca and I approached the counter with the little dog close at our heels.

"Excuse me—" I began.

"Sorry, you're too late," the man snapped, cutting me off.

"Pardon?" I asked, confused.

The woman shook her head. "No more rentals today. Too late. Come back tomorrow."

"That's not why we're here," Becca tried to explain.

"Oh, you mean you want to *buy*?" the woman asked.

"No," I said. "It's not that, either. It's—"

The woman let out an exasperated sigh. "Derek, I can't make anything of what these two are saying. Can't you please handle them?"

"Well, I have no idea what they're doing here either, Deborah," the man answered sharply.

"It might help if you actually listened to what we have to say," Becca pointed out.

They both gaped at us.

"Well, get on with it then," Deborah said. "We don't have all day."

But you do have a major attitude problem, I added silently. *All right, Kayla, keep cool,* I reminded myself. *It's not going to help anything to make them mad at you before you even get a chance to say what you came here to say.*

I cleared my throat. "Actually, we came to talk to you about the Jet Ski area in the ocean by Cayenga Park," I said.

Derek and Deborah glanced at each other quickly.

Derek narrowed his dark eyes and stared at me. "What do you know about that?" he demanded.

Now it was my turn to be confused. "What do you mean? Everybody knows about it. Especially the kids on the kiddie beach right nearby. Which is actually what we want to talk to you about."

"Oh," said Derek, his eyes widening. "The Jet Ski area by the *kiddie beach*! Of course!"

"Yes, that's right," I said. These two sure could be frustrating to talk to. Better get to the point, I decided. "The Jet Skis there are coming really close to the swimmers. In fact, one almost hit me last week."

Deborah raised an eyebrow. "Are you telling me that one of our customers took a Jet Ski inside the swimming area?"

I shook my head. "No, actually, I was just outside the swim zone, on the other side of the buoys, but—"

"Well, then, I'd say *you're* the one who's at fault here," Derek said coolly. "After all, you're the one who wasn't where she was supposed to be."

"Because she was saving a little kid's life!" Becca objected.

At the sound of Becca's raised voice, the little dog on the floor began to growl.

"Don't worry, Salty," Deborah crooned, coming around to the front of the counter to pick up the dog in her arms.

"We're junior park rangers," I explained. "I was lifeguarding that day at the park."

"Well, the park has absolutely no say over the area beyond the buoys," Deborah said, stroking the dog's head. "In fact, that's one of the biggest problems you park people have—interfering where you don't belong." She smiled smugly. "But that can't last forever, you know."

What, exactly, is she trying to say? I wondered. *Is that supposed to be some kind of threat?*

"Look," I said, trying one last time. "I know the area beyond the buoys isn't part of the park. But it's right next to an area where people swim. All I'm asking is that you tell your Jet Ski customers to be careful, and not to drive too close to the buoys."

"And all we're asking is that you keep your nose out of our business," Derek replied sharply.

The dog let out an angry bark.

"My brother's right," Deborah added. "It's very clear, you know. The park is the park, and everything else is fair game. You stay on your side of the buoys, and we'll stay on ours."

I felt anger and frustration welling up inside me.

"Don't you even have any consideration for anyone else?" I said, my voice rising.

Becca put her hand on my arm. "Kayla . . ."

I knew I should probably stop, but I couldn't. I was too upset. "Don't you see that those Jet Skis are obnoxious and annoying, and that some day they might even hurt someone?" The dog started barking hysterically, and I raised my voice to be heard above it. "All you care about is yourselves and your stupid business!" I finished.

Deborah stroked the dog's head. "There, there, Salty," she soothed. She gave me a hard stare. "That's correct," she said coolly. "It is our business. Which gives us the right to ask you to leave the premises immediately."

"Come on, Kayla, let's go," Becca said in a low voice, tugging at my arm.

Angrily I turned to leave. *I can't believe these two,* I thought furiously. *They've got to be two of the most self-centered, uncaring people I've ever met.*

As we reached the door to the shop, Derek called out to us from behind the counter. "And please *don't* bother coming back!"

SIX

"What does it mean to be part of a community?" Ms. Saslow asked from her spot at the front of the room.

It was the following Monday afternoon, and I was sitting next to Alex in our history class. At Harmon you get to choose an elective history course in ninth grade. Alex and I had both chosen Communities, with Ms. Saslow, for this semester.

Jane Armour raised her hand in front of me. "It means the place where you live."

Ms. Saslow nodded slowly. "True, true." She looked around the room. "Is that it?"

I raised my hand. "I think being part of a community means that you have a responsibility to the other people in the community, and they have a responsibility to you," I said.

"So a community is a group of individuals who care about each other's well-being," Ms. Saslow replied.

"Not always," Jennifer Kim pointed out. "I mean, there are lots of people in every community who don't seem to care about anyone else at all."

Isn't that the truth, I thought, remembering the run-in I'd had with the owners of the Salty Dog two days earlier. I raised my hand. "Well, then, being part of a community means that people *should* care about each other," I said.

Ms. Saslow nodded. "What about the community of our classroom? Or our school? Or our town? What should our responsibilities be to one another in those communities?" Then she glanced at her watch. "Oh, dear, we're out of time. I suppose we'll have to continue tomorrow."

We all began gathering our books and papers.

"Oh, wait," Ms. Saslow said. "Let me hand out the research paper assignment before you go." She picked up a stack of papers from her desk and handed them to the first girl in the row to pass back.

When the stack got to me, I took a sheet and handed the rest to Alex. I tucked my notebook under my arm and scanned the assignment as I walked slowly toward the classroom door.

Research Paper Assignment   Ms. Saslow
Due November 30   Communities, grades 9–10
                           Harmon Academy

Research and write a 10–12 page paper on one of the following:

1. Select a historical community, from any time period, and investigate the structures that functioned within it.
or
2. As we have been studying, there are many communities within communities. Think about the community in which you live. What communities exist within that larger community? Select a subcommunity of today (it can be one of which you consider yourself a part, or not) and describe the structures that exist within it.

When preparing your paper on either of the two subjects above, please think about the following:

How is the community organized? Who are the official and unofficial leaders? Do you think this community is a successful one? Why or why not?

A moment later I heard Alex's voice behind me. "What are you going to write about, Kayla?"

I don't know," I answered. "Probably something in the second choice, about a community of today. I don't know what, though." I looked at her. "What about you? What are you going to write your paper on?"

"Gears," she answered.

I stared at her. "Gears?" I laughed a little. Alex is totally into machinery and mechanics. "I'm sorry to have to break this to you, Alex, but I think you're going to have to write about human beings for this one."

Alex laughed. "I meant the Gears chat room on the Internet," Alex explained. "It's part of a web site for people who like to build their own bikes."

"Oh," I said, understanding. "I guess that counts as a community."

"I think it does," Alex agreed. "The way I see it, it's a virtual community, of bike builders who like to talk to each other about the stuff they're interested in."

I nodded. "Makes sense. I wonder what I should write about? It would be fun to do it on something right here in Cayenga."

"You could write about the karate community at your dad's school," Alex offered.

"That's true," I said. "But I just wrote a paper on karate last year for Ms. Cohen. Remember? We had to write about one of our ambitions? I'd like to do it on something different. Since it's a research paper, it would be fun to write about something I'm actually interested in learning about." Suddenly I had an idea. "I know! I can write about Seal Island!"

"But is Seal Island a community?" Alex asked doubtfully. "There aren't exactly any people there."

"No, but the seals are a community," I said. "They probably even have leaders and structures and stuff just like human communities. I could even compare their community to human communities."

"Sounds cool to me," Alex said.

"Do you want to go down to the library in town after school to start on our research?" I asked her.

"No need to," Alex explained. "We can work from the school library."

"I know, but the one in town is so much bigger," I pointed out. "We'll probably find lots more information about seals and the Internet down there."

"Kayla, we can *use* the Internet right here at school to do our research," Alex objected. "A lot of the information we want is probably available on-line."

"That's true. But it's a gorgeous day outside," I said. "I mean, I think it's great that we have so much information right at our fingertips and everything, but you have to admit that nothing on-line can ever beat a walk downtown in the sunshine. Besides," I added, "the town library's on-line, too, so we can always still use the Internet as much as we want for research there."

"Okay, okay, Mother Nature," Alex said good-naturedly. "I know better than to fight with you about this kind of stuff. We can walk downtown to the library after school if that's what you want."

Later that afternoon I carried a stack of books over to a large open desk in the main research room of the town library. The librarian had helped me find several books on marine animals and ocean life. We had even located a thin book on the plants and animals of southern California's offshore islands.

I glanced over to the computer station by the far wall. Alex was hunched over in one of the carrels, working intently. I turned back to my stack of books and removed the top one from the pile. It was called *Ocean Mammals—Man's Cousins in the Sea.*

Whose idea was it to call all of humanity "man"? I wondered for about the millionth time. *I hate it when old books do that. Still, you can't judge a book by its cover, so I guess I'll give it a chance.*

I flipped it open and scanned the table of contents, easily locating "Seals". I turned to the page listed.

But to my surprise, the photograph on the first page of the chapter didn't look very much like the seals I'd seen on Seal Island. The animals in the book were much broader looking, with thick necks and wide bodies. And they were missing their cute little teddy-bear-like earflaps.

I flipped back to the table of contents. There, above the listing for "Seals," I spotted another one, for "Sea Lions." I turned to the appropriate page.

As I did, a piece of pale blue paper torn into a narrow strip fluttered out and landed on the floor. I picked it up and put it on the table. There was some printing on one side, but not enough to make out what the strip was originally from.

```
┌─────────────┐
│ ISS OU      │
│   OF R      │
│      FO     │
│             │
│ OG W        │
│ CEAN        │
│   CA        │
└─────────────┘
```

Probably just a scrap someone was using to mark their place, I thought. I turned to the book.

Of the five species of sea lion, the California sea lion (Z.c. californianus) is the most well-known. It is found along the Pacific coast of North America from Vancouver Island to Mexico. California sea lions are mammals. They are fur-covered, breathe air, bear live young, and nurse their babies. Sea lions, seals, and walruses are all pinnipeds, a group of aquatic mammals. Sea lions are distinct from seals in several ways. Sea lions have earflaps and large, strong front flippers. They are also able to move around on land with relative ease.

So the seals on Seal Island aren't seals at all, I thought incredulously. *They're sea lions! Which means that Seal Island's name is totally wrong!*

I fumbled through the pile of books until I located the thin volume called *The Offshore Islands of Southern California—Flora and Fauna.* I turned to the table of contents and found a listing that said:

Quickly I turned to the page. I was slightly surprised when another narrow strip of blue paper fell out. *It looks as if someone else was researching this same stuff,* I realized. I put the second strip of paper on top of the first one and went back to the book.

The entry for Seal Island was short and mostly talked about the plants that grew there and the colony of sea lions that had lived there for at least sixty years, as far as anyone could tell. At the end of the paragraph I found this:

Seal Island, which has been under the unofficial protection of Cayenga Park since 1965, is somewhat inappropriately named, probably due to misinformation on the part of the general public regarding seals versus sea lions—two marine mammals that are commonly confused.

As the afternoon wore on, I continued to pore through the books, taking notes on all the important sea lion information I could find. As I researched, I learned that female sea lions are called cows, males are bulls, and babies are called pups. I also read that sea lions like to stay together in large groups to protect themselves from predators and from cold weather. I learned that they can live eighteen years or more, and that one was even documented as being thirty years old. According to the books, sea lions are hardly ever found more than ten miles out to sea, and they tend to come back to the same spots year after year to have their babies.

As I was reading, I also discovered several more blue bookmarks like the first two I'd found. It seemed pretty clear that someone else had been looking for a lot of the exact same information I was.

I wonder whose papers these are and how long they've been in here? But there was no way of telling. Whoever it was could have put them in the books last year or last week. *I just hope it's not another girl from Harmon doing her paper on the same subject I chose,* I thought anxiously. It didn't seem too likely. After all, we'd only gotten the assignment that morning. Still, it made me feel kind of funny to think that someone else had been looking for something in all the exact same sections of the exact same books as I had.

SEVEN

"Hey, you guys, you want to stop by the restaurant for a while?" Becca asked. "The seafood special today is marinated octopus."

"You must be kidding," Carson said.

Becca shook her head. "It's good, too."

It was the following afternoon, and we'd all just finished up our stint at the park. I had hoped that Ranger Abe would assign me to the coastal patrol again so I could sneak another peek at Seal Island up close, but when I got to the park after school, my name was listed on the assignment board next to "Campground Welcome Booth."

"I'll come to the restaurant," Sophie offered. "But I'm not too sure about the octopus."

"What's the matter? Are you chicken?" Becca asked with a twinkle in her eye.

"Chicken sounds great," Sophie joked. "How about an order of Barry's chicken nachos? Or doesn't he make that stuff anymore?"

"I'll try the octopus," Carson said with a shrug.

"What about you, Alex?" Becca asked. "Are you strong enough to brave the dreaded eight-armed under-sea monster?"

"Actually, I'd better not go," Alex said. "Kayla and I have this big paper due soon, and I haven't finished my research yet."

"I haven't, either," I said. "Where are you going, the library?"

"Actually, I think I'll go back and use my computer at home," Alex replied. "I want to go on-line in the Gears chat room so I can do some of my own research there."

I nodded. "It's a cool idea to do some of the research directly yourself, and not just rely on other people's information you find in books and on the Internet, I guess." That gave me a great idea. "Hey, maybe I'll take out a boat and go check out Seal Island for a while. I bet it would really help my paper to do some research on the sea lion community there myself."

"I'm sure Ms. Saslow will be totally impressed," Alex said.

I turned to Carson. "We're allowed to take out boats if we want, right?"

She nodded. "Just as long as you sign out the boat and take a life preserver," she said.

"Sorry I can't come with you on this mission, Super-Kayla, but the eight-armed undersea creature awaits me," Becca joked. "Not to mention the yummy lemon-garlic marinade it's sitting in!" She laughed.

"That's okay," I told her. It was true. I was looking forward to just sitting quietly and observing the sea lions.

"Just be careful, Kayla," Carson cautioned. "Remember, there's not that much time left before sunset."

"Yeah," Alex added, "and you should check the weather board by the dock for storm postings before you go, just in case."

I smiled. The sky was completely blue, and there wasn't the slightest breeze. The sun wasn't anywhere near setting. I was sure I would be absolutely fine. But it was nice to know they cared.

•   •   •

Twenty minutes later I sat motionless in a small Cayenga Park boat off the shore of Seal Island, watching as dozens of sea lions dived off the black rocks and splashed in the water.

I easily identified the males, the bulls, by their tremendous size, and the females, or cows, by their smaller, more streamlined bodies. There were several young sea lions as well, some sitting on the rocks watching their parents swim, and a couple in the water playing on their own.

One huge male spent all his time on a gigantic rock that towered above the others. I noticed that although the other sea lions often scuffled for spots on the other rocks, no one ever seemed to go near him.

"Well, it's pretty clear who's king of that rock," I said to myself with a smile.

On cue, as if he knew I was talking about him, King rolled over on his side and stretched out regally in the sun, one flipper dangling off the edge of the rock.

Nearby, two smaller, younger-looking sea lions took turns pushing each other into the water. Watching them, I couldn't help smiling. *They never stop fighting,*

I marveled to myself. I laughed. *Kind of like Sophie and Jason.*

A few yards offshore from where Sophie and Jason were playing, I noticed a mother cow and her pup swimming together, not too far away from me. They were diving under the water over and over again, first the cow, and then the pup. At first I thought they were playing, but then I saw the mother surface with a small fish in her mouth.

She's probably teaching her baby to catch food, I realized.

I continued watching them as they dived. Then, suddenly, the pup went down and didn't surface right away. Its mother dived in and quickly nosed it to the surface.

Look how she pushed the baby up for air just in time, I thought with admiration. *She came to her pup's rescue instinctively when it needed her.* It made me think of the way I had felt that day on the beach with Jeff. Once I realized he was in trouble, I was in the water swimming out toward him before I even had time to think about it. *It was instinct,* I realized, *almost like with the mother sea lion.* I couldn't help wondering if my rescue instinct was still there.

Just then the mother sea lion broke away from her pup and swam cautiously toward the boat as if inspecting me. I had the feeling she was sizing me up, deciding whether I was dangerous or not.

I gazed at the dark eyes looking up at me from the water.

"It's okay," I said softly. "I'm not going to hurt you. Your baby is safe."

She regarded me a moment longer, and then flipped back under the water, bumping my boat slightly with her tail as she turned.

I laughed. "Hey there, Bumper, take it easy or you'll tip me over," I said.

She glanced back at me and did another flip, this time farther away. I laughed again. She almost seemed to be teasing me.

I bent over and trailed my fingertips into the water. "Bumper!" I called softly. "Oh, Bumper!"

The sea lion returned to the boat, swimming by just inches from my fingertips. *It's like she's daring me,* I thought in amazement. *Daring me to reach out to her.*

She came toward me again, and I stretched my hand out ever so slightly. I felt her slick, wet fur graze my fingers as she passed.

"Wow!" I said out loud. *She's starting to trust me. This is incredible!* "Bumper! Bumper!" I called to her again.

This time it was her pup who started eagerly for the boat. Thrilled, I reached out farther.

"Hello there, honey!" I called out happily.

But just then Bumper, who was in the water nearby, let out a deafening bark.

Startled, I jumped back, rocking the boat. I grabbed the side to keep from falling out.

At the sound of the bark, the sea lion pup turned instantly and began swimming toward its mother. Bumper continued barking and swam quickly away from me, leading her child back toward the island.

"Wait!" I cried, feeling disappointment wash over me. "Bumper, come back! I'm not going to hurt your baby!"

But the mother cow didn't stop swimming. I watched as she and the baby reached the island. Bumper nosed her little one ashore and then followed, beaching herself on the wet sand.

I felt a little bad, but I supposed I understood why the mother sea lion had been reluctant to trust me with her baby. *I guess she was just being smart and careful,*

I realized. *And that's probably a good thing as far as sea lion survival goes.* Still, I felt a little disappointed. The baby had been so cute, and it was definitely headed straight for me. *But maybe if I come out here again soon, Bumper will get to know me,* I reasoned. *Once she understands that she can trust me, maybe then she'll let her pup get closer.*

I looked around and suddenly realized that the sun was awfully low in the sky. *I must have been out here watching the sea lions much longer than it seemed,* I thought. *I guess I'd better get back.*

I pulled on the cord to start the little outboard motor. It sputtered for a moment and then died. *I guess Alex has a point about that "easy-start" button thing being a lot easier,* I thought wryly.

I pulled the cord again, and this time the motor started. Reluctantly I turned the boat away from Seal Island and headed back toward shore.

I should bring someone out to see this the way Alex brought me the other day, I thought. *These animals are so great. It would be wonderful if more people had an opportunity to see them in their natural habitat.*

I considered the idea for a moment. Maybe it *was* possible for more people to see them, after all.

EIGHT

Two days later I practically flew up the path to park headquarters after school, my purple paisley backpack bumping on my back as I ran.

Carson, Sophie, and Becca were standing outside the building, studying the assignment board.

"Whoa, Kayla, don't forget to put on the brakes! You sure must be excited to see what part of the park you're working in today," Becca joked.

"I've got this great idea, and I can't wait to tell Ranger Abe about it," I said, out of breath. "Does anyone know where he is?"

"I think he's in his office," Carson offered. "But hang on a minute. What's your idea?"

"And where's Alex?" Sophie asked. "Doesn't she usually walk over here after school with you?"

"She's on her way," I answered, still panting. "She knows all about my idea; I told her in school. But I ran ahead because I wanted to catch Ranger Abe before I had to report to my post in the park." I paused to catch my breath and looked at the three of them. "Okay, here it is. I think the park should make a visitors' observation center on Seal Island."

"Cool idea," Becca commented, nodding.

"You mean so people could see the seals firsthand?" Carson asked.

"Sea lions," I corrected her. "They're actually California sea lions, and not seals at all. Which is exactly why I think there should be a visitors' center on the island."

Sophie looked confused. "You think there should be a visitors' center because they're California sea lions and not seals?"

"No, I mean because people just don't know enough about them," I explained. "You see, I started thinking about how Seal Island got that name because people thought it was covered with seals. That got me to thinking about how there's a lot of stuff people probably don't know about marine mammals. Like what the differences are between seals and sea lions. And how long they live, and what they eat, and how they take care of their babies, and stuff like that. I think that watching the sea lions in their natural habitat would be an amazing attraction for visitors. And it would be good for the sea lions, too, because people would learn more about them."

"But how would park visitors get out to the island?" Sophie asked. "It's all the way out in the ocean."

"There would have to be some kind of big boat," I said.

Carson looked doubtful. "I'm pretty sure Ranger Abe will say there's not enough money in the park budget to do something like that."

"I thought of that, too," I said. "But if the boat charged visitors an extra fee to go out and visit the sea lions, sooner or later it would pay for itself. And my guess is it would be sooner, rather than later. Once people see how cool it is to check out the sea lions on the island, I'm sure there would be tons of customers."

"And if there weren't, we could always put huge ugly signs all over the park that say, 'You are almost

there. The sea lion boat is just around the corner!'"
Becca joked.

Just then, Alex walked up the path to the building.

"Hi, guys. Did Kayla tell you all about her idea?"
she asked. "Kayla, what did Ranger Abe say? Did you
ask him?"

"Not yet," I said. I looked around at my friends.
"Come with me, you guys. You can help me explain it,
okay?"

A few minutes later the five of us stood in Ranger
Abe's office. He sat behind his gray metal desk,
listening, his ranger hat tilted back on his head,
revealing his graying hair.

". . . and so we figure that pretty soon the boat
would pay for itself," I finished.

Ranger Abe leaned forward. "Well, I can see you've
given this a lot of thought, Kayla, and it's a plan I like
very much—"

"Really?" I said, excited.

"Isn't it great?" Sophie said.

"But," Ranger Abe went on, "there's one problem
with it. A problem that, I'm afraid, makes the whole
thing impossible."

My heart sank. "What's that?"

"Seal Island doesn't belong to the park," Ranger Abe said. "It belongs to the town."

"Oh, I know," I said. "But the town has been letting the park rangers take care of it for over thirty years, right?"

Ranger Abe nodded. "That's right. But it's still not park property, technically speaking. Which means that only the town council can decide what happens to it."

"Okay, so maybe we have to present the idea to the town council," Alex offered.

"I'm sure they'd agree to it," Carson put in. "I mean, what reason would they have not to?"

"A *big* reason, I'm afraid," Ranger Abe replied. He paused, frowning for a moment. "From what I've heard, the town council is thinking of taking the island back and selling it."

"Selling it?" I said incredulously. "But to who?"

"Really," Becca joked. "Who would want to buy an island in the middle of the ocean covered with seals—I mean, sea lions?"

"Well, for one thing, it's not quite as covered with sea lions as it used to be," Ranger Abe replied.

"But I was out there with Alex, and she told me there

were tons more sea lions on the island than there were when she was little," I objected.

"Kayla's right," Alex agreed. "There weren't nearly as many of them out there when I was a kid, Ranger Abe."

"For a while the sea lion population *was* growing," Ranger Abe replied. "And it's true that there are still significantly more animals on the island than there were fifteen years ago. But in this past year the numbers have begun to drop noticeably. There are maybe two-thirds as many sea lions now as there were six months ago."

"But what happened to them?" I asked.

Ranger Abe shook his head. "No one knows. Some people believe they may be finding new homes. But as they disappear, the town is reconsidering what to do with the island. They've had an offer from someone to buy it from them, and some council members are beginning to think that's the way to go."

"But who wants to buy it?" Alex asked.

"Does someone actually want to live there?" Sophie wondered.

"No, but someone wants to open a business there,"

Ranger Abe said. "That water-sports rental place in town is proposing to set up an outpost out there."

"The Salty Dog?" I cried. "No way!"

Ranger Abe nodded. "That's what I hear."

"But those people are horrible!" Becca said incredulously.

"Wow," Carson muttered. "Just what Cayenga doesn't need—more Jet Skis."

"They have to be stopped," I said. I looked around at my friends. "We can't let this happen." I thought of Bumper and her baby, and the other sea lions I was coming to know. Where would they all go if a Jet Ski rental outpost were allowed to open on the island? And people on Jet Skis were bound to accidentally kill more sea lions. "We can't let the Salty Dog get away with this!"

NINE

The following afternoon the five of us sat at our favorite window table at the Cayenga Grill, Becca's family's restaurant. It was Friday, and we had all agreed to head over there after working in the park to discuss the Seal Island situation.

"I really can't stand the thought of those snobby obnoxious people from the Salty Dog getting their paws on Seal Island," Becca said. Then she grinned. "Ha ha. Get it? *Dog? Paws?*"

There was a little halfhearted laughter.

"I guess no one's really in the mood for jokes," Becca said in a low voice.

"There must be something we can do," I said for

what felt like the hundredth time since I'd heard the news from Ranger Abe the afternoon before. I shook my head. "Can you imagine what it would be like with even more Jet Skis roaring around offshore? It'll be almost impossible to find a peaceful spot on any of the park's coast."

"Do you really think the town council will let this happen?" Sophie asked. "I mean, don't they care about the sea lions?"

Alex sighed. "From what Ranger Abe said, they seem to think the sea lions are moving away."

I shook my head. "I definitely don't believe that. According to my research, sea lions like to return year after year to the same spot to have their babies. Seal Island is perfect for them. Why would they suddenly leave? They've been there for generations."

"But then what's happening to them?" Carson asked. "Ranger Abe says there are a lot less of them now than there were last year."

No one said anything. I had the feeling no one knew what to say.

Just then Becca's stepdad, Barry, walked over to the table. His white chef's apron was stained with various liquids and juices, and his curly brown hair was tucked back in a white kerchief. In his arms was a tray with several steaming soup bowls on it.

"All right," Barry said cheerfully. "Who wants to be the first to try my newest special?" He raised his eyebrows. "It's conch stew."

"Conch?" Carson repeated. "Conch? As in those giant snail-like things in the pretty pink shells?"

Barry laughed. "Well, yes. Although I didn't include any of the pink shell part in the stew. Hope that isn't too much of a disappointment."

The table was silent.

Barry looked disappointed. "What, no takers?" He sniffed at the tray. "Gee, and I was sure this delicious aroma would win everyone over."

"It smells great, Barry," Becca assured him. "I guess we're just not feeling that enthusiastic right now."

"What's up?" Barry set the tray down on a nearby table. "Trouble in the park?"

"Not exactly," Alex answered.

"We just found out that the town's thinking of selling Seal Island," I explained.

"Oh, yeah, that's that little island out there with the other two, right? I heard about that," Barry said, nodding. "Great idea, don't you think?"

"Great idea?" Becca burst out. "You must be kidding!"

Barry looked surprised. "No? Why not? I heard down at the Cayenga Small Business Owners Association that a lot of people are really excited about it. There's a proposal going before the town council next Tuesday."

"Tuesday!" I said, alarmed. We didn't have much time.

"A lot of people seem to like the idea," Barry went on. "They say it'll probably attract a lot of visitors. And more tourists means more customers for Cayenga businesses. Businesses like ours."

"Barry!" Becca cried, sounding horrified.

"The plan might sound good for businesses," I said. "But it would be terrible for the colony of sea lions that lives out there."

Barry's eyes widened. "You mean there are actually sea lions on that island?"

I nodded. "They've been there for sixty years, maybe longer. They have their babies out there and everything."

Barry scratched his chin. "Well, that sheds a different light on things entirely."

Just then the door to the restaurant opened, and a familiar-looking man walked in. It took me a moment to recognize him as Carl Conti, the man from the fish stand. Mr. Conti wasn't dressed in his regular fishing gear, but had on a simple T-shirt and jeans. He walked over to Barry and put a hand on his shoulder.

"Mr. Conti!" Barry greeted him warmly.

"Mr. Chef," Mr. Conti returned the greeting. "You're just the man I wanted to see. I'm letting you be the first to know about the new catch today. Are you interested in some shark meat?"

"For sure," Becca's stepfather replied. "I'd love to do barbecued shark steaks for tomorrow. Is it fresh?"

"Fresh as it gets," Mr. Conti assured him. "I just pulled in a big one this morning."

"A shark?" Becca said, her eyes widening. "You caught a real shark? In this ocean, right here?"

"That's right," Mr. Conti said. He narrowed his eyes a little. "Hey, you look familiar. Weren't you down by my stand last week?"

Becca nodded.

"That's my stepdaughter, Becca," Barry explained.

"How far out did you catch this shark, exactly?" Sophie asked in a worried-sounding voice.

Barry grinned. "The girls are all junior rangers at the park. They do a lot of lifeguarding and boating, so they spend some time in the water."

"Don't worry, it wasn't in one of the swimming beaches or anything," Mr. Conti replied. "I snagged her out by Gull Island."

That made me think of something. "Excuse me, Mr. Conti," I said. "But do sharks normally eat sea lions?" *Maybe that could explain the shrinking number of sea lions on Seal Island in the past year,* I reasoned. *Maybe there have been more sharks in the area lately or something.*

"Another spectator from the fish stand," Mr. Conti said, recognizing me. "Yes, sharks occasionally eat sea lions. But not too often. Not often enough, if you ask me."

I was stunned. "What did you say?"

"Well, this may be hard for you to hear, but the sea lion is one of the fisherman's worst enemies," Mr. Conti replied. "They're notorious thieves. Steal all your fish from the nets if you're not careful." He chuckled a little. "Sorry to say it, Mr. Chef, but if it were up to me, I'd have you serving sea lion sandwiches every day of the week."

"Well, I'm afraid I can't help you out with that one," Barry said, steering Mr. Conti away from our table. "Thanks for letting me know about the shark, though. I'll stop by the dock first thing in the morning."

I stared at Mr. Conti's back as he walked toward the door.

"I can't believe he said that stuff," I said, my throat tense with anger. I thought of Bumper and her baby, playing in the water together. "No one who ever watched a mother sea lion with her pup could ever say such a cruel thing."

"It did seem pretty heartless," Carson agreed.

"Besides," I continued, "fishermen and their nets do much more serious damage to sea lions than sea lions do to them."

"How's that?" Alex asked, leaning forward.

"I read that when sea lions get caught in fishing nets they can drown and die," I explained.

"They can drown?" Becca said. "But they live in the water. Aren't they really good swimmers?"

"They're excellent swimmers," I responded. "But they're mammals, which means they need to breathe air, like we do. They generally only stay underwater for a minute at a time. It's possible for them to stay under for up to fifteen minutes if they have to, but if they're tangled in a net and can't get free, that might not be enough." *There's so much for people to learn about these animals,* I thought again. *Which is exactly why we really need that visitors' center.*

If only there were some way to convince the town council of that, I thought. My heart sank, thinking of Mr. Conti's words. *If the rest of Cayenga feels the way he does, the visitors' center has no chance at all,* I realized. *Not unless we do something fast. But what?*

TEN

The following night I lay in Alex's bed, fingering the salmon-pink bedspread and staring up at the ceiling. Alex was curled in her army-green sleeping bag on the floor beside the bed, breathing deeply. But somehow I just couldn't seem to get to sleep.

Alex had invited me to use her computer to finish the research for my paper and then sleep over. I generally do all my Internet stuff on the computers at school, but since this was a weekend and school was closed, Alex had offered me her totally amazing computer setup. Her parents were both out of town on business, and I think she wanted to have some company for the night. Even though there are a couple of maids who live in the house, and a cook who sleeps over when Alex and her younger sister, Trish, are home on their own, it's still a really big house. Besides, the cook and the maids stay in a whole separate wing, so I could understand why Alex might get a little lonely.

Like I said, Alex has an unbelievable computer system. Meanwhile, I must be the only girl in the Harmon Academy ninth grade who doesn't have a computer at home at *all*. And—okay, you may have to brace yourself for this one—I *know* I must be just about the only girl in the entire school who doesn't have a television.

The funny thing is, I don't really mind it. I've always been more into reading and writing in my journal and stuff than watching TV anyway. And the whole old-fashioned back-to-basics thing kind of seems to go with the atmosphere in my house, somehow. Maybe it's because it used to be a barn a long time ago. There's a lot of open space and sunlight and stuff. My mom's art studio and our living room and dining room are really all one big space, in the main section of the barn. My bedroom and my parents' are upstairs, in what used to be the hayloft. Somehow it's hard to imagine how it would all work out if one person were watching TV while someone else was playing a noisy computer game. The way the sound carries inside the barn, it definitely wouldn't be very peaceful.

But it was extremely peaceful in Alex's room right now. Almost too peaceful. If I had to watch the rippling reflection of the pool lights from outside on the ceiling for one more minute, I just knew I was going to burst.

I climbed out of bed. Stepping carefully over Alex, I made my way to the window seat built into the far wall. I sat down in the corner of the window seat, tucked my knees up to my chest, and pulled my night-shirt down over them. I looked out the window.

Directly below me was the roof of the veranda and, beyond that, the pool.

Are those pool lights really supposed to stay on all night? I wondered. Somehow it seemed like a pretty major waste of energy, especially since no one was even awake to see the pool. No one but me, that is.

Past the pool the landscape dropped off sharply in a series of steep cliffs leading down to the ocean. The moon was nearly full, and I could see the dark water and the whitecaps glistening in the distance.

As my eyes adjusted I realized I could make out the Three Sisters against the horizon. There they were:

Surf Island, Gull Island, and at the northernmost tip, Seal Island.

I smiled to myself. *I wonder what Bumper and her baby are up to right now. I suppose they're probably asleep,* I thought. I gazed out at the island, imagining the mother seal and her pup curled up for the night.

Then, suddenly, I spotted something odd. It looked like a small flash of light near the southern edge of the island. I sat up more alertly, and kept watching.

A moment later I saw it again. This time the light lasted longer—a few seconds—and bobbed a little. I froze. It seemed as though someone was walking around out there with a flashlight.

But who? I wondered. *And why?*

I sat perfectly still, not moving my eyes from the spot where I had last seen the light. I waited, but nothing happened.

Just when I was about to give up, I spotted a light on the other side of the island, to the north. This light was brighter and continuous; it didn't flicker. It took me a moment to realize that this light, too, was moving, moving steadily in fact—away from the island.

It's a boat! I realized as its dark shape became visible against the horizon. *But what would a boat be doing out there at this hour?* I wondered. I shivered a little thinking about it. There was no doubt about it. Someone was sneaking around on Seal Island in the middle of the night—and from what I knew already, I had a pretty strong feeling that whoever it was was up to no good.

ELEVEN

"Are you absolutely sure about what you saw, Kayla?" Alex asked me the next morning.

I nodded. "Positive."

"Well, it definitely sounds weird to me." Alex grabbed a box of cornflakes off the kitchen counter and picked up a couple of cereal bowls and spoons. "Can you get the milk, Kayla?"

I walked across the kitchen to the enormous silver refrigerator and opened the door. It took me a moment to find the milk, probably because it was in a special cubbyhole designed to fit the carton and built into the door.

I followed Alex out of the kitchen, through the

music room, and onto the veranda. The view was to the north, and I could see Seal Island to my left as I sat down at the little round table opposite Alex. Staring out at the ocean through the morning mist, what I'd seen the night before seemed unreal, almost like a dream. But I was certain it wasn't.

Alex poured some cereal into each of our bowls. "I wonder why someone would be out there in the middle of the night."

"Probably because they didn't want anyone to see what they were doing," I said. I shook my head. "Alex, I have a really bad feeling about this. Maybe we should go out there and check out the island ourselves."

"Okay, sure," Alex agreed. "I'll go with you, Kayla. We can head to the park right after breakfast. Who knows, maybe we can find some evidence of whatever was going on there last night."

An hour later Alex and I stood at the little dock in the park where the boats are kept.

"Here, let's take this one," I said, pointing to the nearest boat. "Sign us out. I'll get some life preservers, okay?"

I hurried into the small boathouse, where a ranger I

recognized from around the park sat behind a wooden desk, reading a newspaper. The badge on her green uniform shirt identified her as Ranger Melinda Clemente.

"Hi," I greeted her. "We're going to take out a boat, okay? My friend and I, that is. We're both junior rangers."

"Oh, sure, GIRLS R.U.L.E., right?" She smiled. "Go ahead. Just sign out and take life jackets. Which direction are you headed?"

"Over toward the Three Sisters," I said. "Seal Island, to be exact." Then I thought of something. "You don't know of anyone else who may have taken a boat out that way recently, do you? Like last night, maybe?"

Ranger Clemente shook her head. "Not from here, at least. We close up at five o'clock so no boats go out after that."

"Okay, thanks," I said.

"Since you're headed south, it might be a good idea to keep an eye out for weather conditions," Ranger Clemente advised. "There's a big storm on its way up from Mexico, but they don't expect it to hit our area until tomorrow. Tonight at the earliest. You shouldn't have any big problems, but the water may be a little choppier than usual."

"Okay, sure thing," I told her. I grabbed two life preservers from the stack against the wall and headed outside.

Alex was waiting for me by the boat. We strapped on our life preservers and climbed in.

"The ranger inside said that there's a storm on its way up the coast," I told Alex. "It's not supposed to hit till tomorrow, though, so we should be okay."

"Okay, good," Alex replied. She started the motor. "Next stop, Seal Island!"

As we approached Seal Island, I squinted and scanned the dark rocks, searching for a sign of—something. I wasn't sure what. We drew closer, and I could see the sea lions lying on the rocks and diving in the water. Ranger Clemente was right; the water was a little rougher than usual. But it didn't seem to bother the sea lions at all. They dived and swam in the area near the island as always, catching fish and fighting battles over rocks.

Alex cut the motor and I scanned the scene. Suddenly I was struck by the thought that something looked different, somehow. I couldn't place exactly what it was at first.

But then I realized. "Where's King?" I said with a gasp.

"What?" Alex asked.

"King," I said again, my eyes frantically searching the island and the water. "He's this great big sea lion who always lies on that rock up there. But he's gone!"

"Maybe he moved to a new rock," Alex suggested. She pointed to another large bull by the pebbly shore. "There. Is that him?"

I shook my head. "King is much bigger. And he's always on that rock. He's definitely disappeared." I began to take stock of the other sea lions. Was it my imagination, or were there fewer of them than there had been the last time I went to the island?

I spotted Sophie and Jason, roughhousing together as usual. Nearby a couple of cows I recognized were with their pups.

Then I saw Bumper's baby, sitting on a low rock looking out to sea. *But where's Bumper? Maybe she left her pup to get some food,* I thought, my heart full of hope.

I scanned the water. No sign of her. I couldn't find Bumper anywhere!

"Alex, there's definitely something very wrong here," I told her, my voice shaking. There's a cow, a mother sea lion, missing, and she's left her pup behind."

Alex looked concerned. "Are you serious?"

I nodded. I couldn't even speak. I felt frantic. Where was Bumper? What had happened to her?

I stared at Bumper's little pup helplessly. *Poor little thing. All alone like that, just waiting for its mother to come back.* I longed to take the boat to the island to try to catch the baby sea lion in my arms. But I knew better. *Wild animals are always better off if they don't have human contact,* I told myself. *Besides, the pup probably wouldn't even come to me. After all, Bumper taught it to stay away.*

I tried to tell myself that everything would be okay. Maybe Bumper would return. Besides, hadn't I read in one of those books at the library that sometimes pups that are left alone are cared for by other mothers? Maybe someone would adopt Bumper's pup.

I told myself all these things, but none of it helped. Seeing Bumper's baby all alone made me feel like my heart was going to break.

TWELVE

Later that day Alex, Becca, Carson, Sophie, and I stood in a huddle not far from Mr. Conti's fish stand.

"What's going on, Kayla?" Sophie asked. "You sounded really upset on the phone."

"Really," Becca agreed. She grinned. "I know you're not here to shop for fish, so what is it?"

"Why did you and Alex want us all to meet here?" Carson asked.

"Alex and I went out to Seal Island this morning," I explained quickly. "There's definitely something strange going on out there. Some sea lions are missing, and I'm sure they didn't leave because they wanted to. One of them was a mother with a young pup. I know there's no way she would have abandoned her pup on purpose."

"Kayla also saw some lights out on the island last night after dark," Alex added. "We think it was someone with a flashlight and a boat."

Sophie's eyes widened. "Wow. Do you think whoever it was did something with the sea lions?"

I nodded. "I'm almost sure of it. And I think I have a feeling who it might have been," I added.

"Let me guess," Carson said. "The people from the Salty Dog?"

"You got it," I answered.

Alex nodded. "It makes sense. After all, the more sea lions that disappear from the island, the easier it's going to be for the Salty Dog to get their Jet Ski proposal approved by the town council."

"I knew that Deborah and Derek were trouble as soon as I met them," Becca grumbled.

"So let's report them or something!" Sophie put in eagerly.

"We can't," I said. "Not without evidence."

"What about the boat you saw?" Sophie suggested. "Couldn't that be the evidence?"

"Do you think you could identify the boat if you saw it again, Kayla?" Carson asked.

"I don't know," I answered doubtfully. "It was late at night. All I really saw was the light on it, and a dark shape."

"That may still give us something to go on," Alex pointed out. "If the owners of the Salty Dog have a boat of the same shape and size, with a light in the same spot, it could at least be a start."

"Either way, I think it's time to do some serious snooping around the Salty Dog," I said.

"But how can we?" Becca asked. "Deborah and Derek told us never to come back, Kayla. Remember?"

I nodded. "But they don't know Carson, Sophie, and Alex at all," I pointed out.

"Good thinking," Carson agreed. "Maybe the three of us can pretend to be customers or something."

"Fine," I said. "You guys just keep them distracted while Becca and I check around the place, okay?"

Alex nodded. "Sure thing."

"Maybe you and I will find just the piece of evidence we're looking for, Kayla," Becca said.

"Let's hope so," I replied. "We don't have much

time. The town council meeting is the day after tomorrow."

And Bumper's baby may have even less time than that, I added silently.

"They're closed!" Carson said in surprise.

"Well, I, for one, am relieved," Becca commented. "I definitely wasn't looking forward to hiding out from Deborah and Derek. Not after the way they threw us out last time."

I walked up to the building and squinted through the screening of one of the windows. The inside of the store was dim and silent.

I turned to face the others with a shrug. "I guess we can all take a look around, then."

"Let's check the back for a boat," Alex suggested.

We walked around the building. Beyond the Jet Skis and windsurfers chained up on the back lawn was a small hill leading down to the water. Sure enough, at the base of the hill was a small dock with a sleek blue speedboat tied to it.

We all hurried over to the boat.

"Kayla, do you think this is the boat you saw?" Sophie asked eagerly.

I stared at the boat. "It could be, but I don't know. It was really far away, and it was dark."

"Wait!" Carson said. "I think something's coming—a car! I felt a vibration in the ground with my feet."

As she finished speaking, I heard it. A car was approaching on the other side of the building.

"It's probably Deborah and Derek," I said nervously. I definitely had the idea that Deborah and Derek wouldn't be too pleased to find us sneaking around behind the Salty Dog and checking out their boat. *Besides,* I reasoned, *if they are in fact the ones who've been messing with the sea lions on the island, it's probably not a good idea to let them know that we're onto them.*

"The only way out of here is the way we came," Alex said, looking around. "We'll have to pass right by the Salty Dog. They'll see us for sure."

"I know," Sophie said quickly. "Let's do the customer act, like we talked about before. Alex, Carson, and I will go in the store and pretend we want to rent something, and while we've got their attention, Kayla and Becca can sneak around front."

"But they'll see us coming from back here," Alex

pointed out. "If we're customers, what are we doing coming from behind the store?"

"We'll tell them we wanted to check out the Jet Skis first," Sophie said eagerly. "Come on, you guys. Let's do it before it's too late and they catch us all back here."

"Sophie's right. You guys go," I agreed. "Becca and I will wait here for a couple of minutes and then sneak back up the hill. We'll all meet by Conti's afterward."

Becca and I watched as Sophie, Carson, and Alex made their way back up the hill. After a few moments the two of us followed.

My heart was beating hard in my chest as Becca and I crept toward the building. I could hear voices coming from inside. A few yards from the back of the store, I crouched down in the grass and motioned Becca to do the same. Together we crawled toward the building on our knees, keeping our heads below the level of the store's rear windows so we wouldn't be seen.

We stopped under a slightly open window and waited.

I heard a muffled voice I recognized as Derek's. "Well, what is it exactly that you're looking for?"

"A Jet Ski," Alex answered. "We want to rent one for the day."

Deborah let out a laugh. "All three of you are going to use one Jet Ski?" she said mockingly. "That will be cozy."

"No, no, we each want to rent one," Sophie said. "What colors do they come in?"

"All of our Jet Skis are blue," Deborah said haughtily. "Salty Dog blue. It's our trademark color."

Becca leaned closer to me. "When should we make a run for it?" she whispered.

"In a minute," I answered. "Let me peek in and see which direction they're facing."

Slowly I straightened my legs just a bit, bringing my eyes to the level of the window just above us. To my surprise, the window that we were under didn't open onto the inside of the store at all, but to a small office cubicle behind the store. The office contained a desk, a file cabinet, and a telephone. Lying asleep curled up in the desk chair was Salty, Deborah and Derek's little dog.

Becca tugged on the leg of my jeans. "Come on," she whispered. "Those guys are leaving. We have to go."

"In a minute," I whispered back. "I want to check something out."

The desk in the office had several piles of papers on it. *If I could just open this window a little wider,* I thought, *I'm sure I'd be able to reach the papers on the desk.*

I stood up. Becca tugged frantically at my leg, trying to pull me back down.

"It's okay," I said. "They can't see us here. Come on up and see for yourself."

Slowly Becca stood up.

"See?" I whispered, pointing at the window. "It's their office. Deborah and Derek's. And I bet the evidence we need is somewhere inside." I pushed at the window frame, and it let out a creak. Salty opened his eyes and looked up at me through the window.

"Kayla, you're crazy!" Becca hissed. "What if they hear you?"

I shoved at the window again, and it opened a little. Salty let out a low growl.

"Sssshhhh! Be quiet!" I whispered to the dog.

"Kayla! What are you doing?" Becca hissed. "We have to get out of here."

"Just wait," I said. "I have to get something first."

I had to admit, I was just as scared as Becca. But I also knew we had no choice. I had to get a look at some of those papers. Maybe there was something in there about Seal Island.

I bent down and stretched my arm through the small opening in the window. Then I bent my elbow and angled my forearm down, toward the desk. I felt some papers in my hand, and I closed my fist around them. Salty began to bark.

"I think I got something!" I whispered excitedly to Becca, pulling the papers back through the window.

But Becca didn't answer. She was staring ahead of her, speechless, looking at something on the other side of the window. I turned my head to see what it was.

There, standing over the desk and glaring back at me, was Derek.

THIRTEEN

"May I *help* you?" Derek asked, his voice tight with anger.

"Um, I—" *Think of something fast, Kayla. Come on, stay on your toes.* "I w-was looking for something," I blurted out finally. "Something I lost." *Oh, great,* I thought. *That was really terrific. Brilliant. Like you could have possibly lost something inside that office while you were outside.*

"Well, I guess you found it, right, Kayla?" Becca said nervously beside me. "So we can go now. Thank you very much." She took my arm.

"Wait just a minute," Derek commanded.

I froze.

"I thought I told you two never to come back here," Derek continued. "And now I find you breaking into private property and rummaging through my papers? I have a good mind to call the police."

I swallowed hard. *This would be pretty hard to explain to the police. Not to mention my parents, once the police call them.*

"Please don't do that," Becca begged. "We didn't mean any harm."

"Well, then, exactly what were you doing?" Derek demanded.

Helplessly I glanced down at the paper in my hand.

DON'T MISS OUR FALL SPECIAL!!!

GET TWO DAYS OF RENTAL ON A JET SKI OR WINDSURFER
FOR THE PRICE OF ONE

SALTY DOG WATER SPORTS
566 OCEAN VIEW ROAD
CAYENGA

"Well, actually, we heard about the special you were having," I said. "I had one of these flyers, but I lost it.

So I came to get another one." I managed to smile. "I have a friend who really wants to rent a windsurfer."

"That's right," Becca said, backing me up. "Our friend loves windsurfing. We just can't get her to stop sometimes. Well, anyway, we'll give her the flyer and send her back here. Thanks again for everything."

Before Derek could say another word, Becca grabbed my arm and we took off around the side of the building.

We ran down Ocean View Road toward the harbor as fast as we could and didn't stop until we reached Conti's, where Alex, Sophie, and Carson were waiting for us.

"What happened to you guys?" Alex said.

"Really. We thought you were going to sneak by while we were inside," Sophie added.

"We stopped to try to nab some evidence," I explained breathlessly, my heart still pounding.

"But instead we were the ones who got nabbed—by Derek," Becca said.

"What's that in your hand?" Carson asked, pointing to the blue flyer I still clutched tightly in my fist. "The evidence?"

"No, it's nothing," I answered. "Just a dumb flyer. I didn't get anything at all."

I glanced down at the flyer in my hand again. *Or did I?*

FOURTEEN

"Wait a minute! Wait a minute!" I said, staring down at the blue flyer in my hand.

"Kayla, what's going on?" Carson asked. "Why do you keep looking at that ad?"

"Don't tell me the Salty Dog's advertising is actually starting to work on you," Becca said.

Could it be? I racked my brain, trying to remember. *What did it look like?*

Wordlessly I began to fold the sheet of paper. I folded it once lengthwise and then again.

"Kayla, what are you doing?" Alex asked.

"Looks like maybe it's origami to me," Becca joked. "What are you going to make, a bird?"

"I think I'm going to make a bookmark," I answered, still concentrating. I folded a couple more times, and then ripped along the folds.

I searched the strips of paper and held up one triumphantly.

```
ISS OU

 OF R

   FO

OG W

CEAN

  CA
```

"That's it!" I said.

"I have to say I'm not that impressed," Becca said. "Are you sure you can't do a bird?"

I turned to look at the four of them. "When I went to the town library to do my research for my paper, I found a bunch of slips of paper marking practically every sea lion section of every book! This looks exactly like the papers I found!" I announced. "Someone else left them there. Someone who was researching sea lions, just like I was."

"I get it!" Sophie said excitedly. "You think it was the people from the Salty Dog!"

"And that they just used one of their flyers to make the markers," Carson said, nodding.

"But why would they be researching sea lions?" Alex asked.

"Who knows?" I said. "There could be tons of reasons. But I bet they all have to do with Seal Island."

"But now what do we do?" Carson asked. "This isn't exactly the kind of evidence we can take to the town council. I mean, researching sea lions at the library isn't a crime."

"I know," I said glumly. I sighed. "This is so frustrating. We all know that the Salty Dog is up to no good. And now I'm almost positive that must have been their boat out there on the island last night."

"But there's no way to prove it," Alex pointed out.

"You're right," I admitted. But I wasn't ready to give up yet. I turned to Alex. "Tell me, do you think we could land one of those little park boats on Seal Island?"

"You mean and get off there and walk around?" she

answered. "Probably. It's pretty rocky, but whoever was there last night did it. Why?"

"I just want to get a closer look," I said. "I have a feeling we may have missed something."

Forty-five minutes later the five of us stood outside the park boathouse, staring at the sign on the board.

CLOSED EARLY DUE TO
INCLEMENT WEATHER

"Too bad," Carson said.

"Maybe we can go out to the island tomorrow instead," Sophie suggested.

I shook my head. "I'm going now."

"Kayla, you can't," Alex objected. "The boathouse is closed. There's a storm on its way up from Mexico, remember?"

I gazed at the sky. It was gray and overcast, but it looked far from stormy. "It's not supposed to hit until tomorrow," I reminded Alex. "If we wait, we might not be able to go to the island at all." I paused. "I'm worried about the sea lions. And I'm worried that the town council will have its meeting on Tuesday and pass the Salty Dog proposal unless we come up with something in time." I looked at my friends. "I'll only go for a little while. Just to check things out. You guys don't have to come."

"I'm going with you," Alex said. "You're going to need help if you expect to land a boat on that island."

"I'll go, too," Carson said. "It's always safer to travel in threes."

"Okay, make that fours," said Becca.

"Well, I'm certainly not going to stay here all by myself!" Sophie objected.

"All right, then, we'll all go," I said. "Can we all fit in one boat?"

"There's a slightly larger one at the end of the dock," Alex said. "Let's take that."

We hurried over to the boat. Although large enough, it didn't have an "easy-start" motor, but we didn't have time to look for another boat.

"What about life preservers?" Carson asked.

"They're in the boathouse," I pointed out. "We can't get to them."

"Is that safe?" Sophie asked doubtfully.

"What could be safer than a boat full of certified lifeguards?" Becca said with a grin.

"We *are* all strong swimmers," Alex agreed.

"If the weather gets too bad we can always head back," Carson added.

"Okay, let's go for it," Sophie said.

The wind was picking up a bit. I held my hair away from my face as I climbed into the boat. One by one the rest of the group climbed in after me. Alex took her usual spot, in the back by the motor.

Carson and I untied the boat and Alex pulled the cord to start the motor. We sped out away from the dock, headed southwest—toward Seal Island.

I couldn't help noticing that the clouds were darker and heavier now. The wind was stronger, and I felt a chill through my flannel shirt. The waves were getting rougher, and as the little boat bounced along, I felt the spray of the chilly water.

As we approached the island I could see that the sea lions were all on the rocks, huddled together against the wind.

"Wow, look at them!" Sophie said.

"What are they doing?" Becca asked.

"Protecting themselves against the weather," I told them. "Look, there isn't one of them in the water. It's almost as if they know a storm is on its way, and they're getting prepared."

"Speaking of getting prepared, the water's starting to get awfully rough," Carson said. "Everybody probably better hang on."

We all gripped the sides of the boat.

"I don't know if I can land in this surf!" Alex called from her spot by the motor. "The shore of the island is so rocky. I don't want to smash the boat!"

I nodded. "Okay," I called back. I was disappointed, but I definitely didn't want us to have an accident.

"I can try to get a little closer so we can have a better look, though," Alex said.

The boat veered closer to the island. I leaned forward, looking for any sign of whoever might have been there the night before. But all I saw were the sea lions, their dark fur glistening on the wet rocks. I wondered where Bumper's baby was. But in the dim light, and with the sea lions huddled the way they were, it was impossible to tell where one animal ended and the next began.

"Can we go around the island?" I asked Alex. "Maybe we'll find something on the other side."

"I'll see what I can do," Alex promised.

We started to circle the island. As we approached the other side, away from the mainland and toward the open sea, the wind got even stronger. I gripped the side of the boat and squinted in the fading light.

"Wow, it's like a whole different island!" Sophie exclaimed.

I saw what she meant. This side of the island was much rockier than the other, with several caves and grottoes. Parts of the island were underwater here, and several irregularly shaped, jagged rock formations jutted out of the water just offshore. There were no sea lions visible anywhere. I could definitely understand why the animals preferred the other side. The rocks over here were sharper and offered very little space to sit. The surf was rougher, as well, and the waves crashed violently against the shore.

"Well, it's definitely impossible to land on this side in this weather," Alex said. "And the storm clouds look like they're really moving in. I guess we should probably go."

I nodded reluctantly. "Maybe the storm will pass by tomorrow and we can try again."

As Alex turned the boat, the motor suddenly stopped. Everything was silent, except for the crashing of the surf against the rocks. The boat was jostled by the rough waves.

"What happened?" Becca asked.

"The motor died," Alex replied. She pulled the cord. It sputtered and then went out again. The boat began drifting toward a jagged column of rock protruding from the water.

There was a flash of lightning, followed by a clap of thunder. Rain began to fall.

"I think we'd better get out of here," I said worriedly.

"I'm trying!" Alex said. She pulled the cord again. The motor coughed and fell silent. "I think it's flooded," she said. "It won't start."

The rain was coming down harder now. My shirt and jeans were soaked through. The wind was whipping. I shivered. Another flash of lightning streaked the sky.

The boat bounced on the rough waves like a tiny toy. And we were headed straight for the rock formation!

"We're going to hit that rock!" Sophie cried.

"Alex, can't you fix the motor?" Carson asked hopefully.

"Not in the rain in the middle of the ocean with no tools," Alex answered, her voice tense.

The waves were pushing us closer to the rock. I could see its dark shape looming beyond the thick curtain of gray rain. I knew we had to do something. But what?

"Quick!" I yelled, leaning over the side of the boat. "Everybody paddle!"

We all bent over and stuck our hands into the water. I paddled as furiously as I could, and I could see Becca doing the same right beside me.

"I've only got one arm to paddle with!" Sophie cried.

"It's no use!" Alex called from the other side of the boat. "We're no match for the current!"

I sat up and stared in horror at the rock formation, which seemed to be growing before my eyes. *We're going to smash right into that thing, and there's nothing we can do!*

Suddenly a huge wave splashed over the side of the boat. I felt the boat lurch suddenly and heard a splintering sound. I heard screams and splashes, and I felt myself lose my balance and fall.

The next thing I knew, there was nothing around me but water. Water in my ears, my eyes, my nose, my lungs. I was surrounded by darkness.

I felt myself sinking . . . down, down, down . . .

FIFTEEN

I continued sinking, my clothes weighing me down, my shoes like bricks.

Go up! Go up! I told myself frantically. *Find the surface!*

I pushed hard against the water, kicking my heavy feet and thrusting myself upward.

Finally my head burst through to the surface. I gulped the air, my lungs aching, my eyes stinging from the salt. The rain was still pouring down, and I couldn't see anything around me.

Where is everybody else? I thought. *Where is the boat?*

"Help!" I cried. A wave hit me in the face, forcing

water into my throat. I coughed and spat. "Help!" I yelled again.

"Kayla?" a voice came from not too far off.

"Becca? Where are you?" I called.

"Over here!" Her voice was coming from my left.

"Are you on the boat?" I asked.

"No," she answered, her voice coming closer. "I'm right here. Carson's here, too. I think the boat sank."

My heart leaped into my throat. *The boat sank? Then where were Alex and Sophie?*

Becca and Carson appeared beside me, treading water.

"Where's the island?" Carson asked. "Can anyone see it?"

"It's raining too hard," I said, moving my arms and legs to stay afloat. My teeth were chattering. We had to get out of that water somehow.

Just then I thought I heard something. It was a distant sound. Like barking.

"What's that?" Becca asked fearfully.

"It's the sea lions!" I replied. "Come on. We can follow the sound to the island." I motioned to Carson with one hand. "Carson, follow us."

The three of us swam together through the dark

churning waves as Becca and I continued listening for the distant barking of the sea lions. Finally the island appeared through the mist, directly in front of us.

"Hey, you guys, over here!" a familiar voice called. It was Alex. She was clinging to a rock at the edge of the shore.

We all started toward her, swimming side by side. When we reached the rock, we grabbed on beside Alex. Slowly, one by one, we pulled ourselves onto the rock. We were all dripping wet and shivering.

"I think we lost the boat," Alex reported. She looked worried. "Has anyone seen Sophie?"

I shook my head.

"Sophie!" Becca called out over the pounding surf. "Sophie! Where are you?"

"Did anyone see what happened to her when we hit the rock?" Carson asked worriedly.

"It all happened too fast," Alex said. "One minute I was paddling over the side, and the next minute I was in the water."

I felt fear gripping at my heart. *What if Sophie's not okay? What if we can't find her? She's got that cast on her arm. What if she can't swim with it?*

I cupped my hands to my mouth. "Sophie!" I called between chattering teeth.

But the storm and the ocean were too loud, and the wind was blowing directly onto us. *She'll never hear us unless she's right nearby.*

Come on, Kayla, I told myself. *Use some power. Just like in karate.* I took a deep breath, feeling the oxygen fill my entire body. Instantly my shivering stopped.

"SOOOPHIEEEEEE!" I bellowed, forcing the sound out of my gut and up through my throat.

"Over here!" a faint voice answered, carried by the wind.

"That was her!" Becca said excitedly.

"She answered?" Carson asked eagerly.

"It sounded like it came from that way," Alex volunteered, pointing to our right.

I stood up on the rock, careful to keep my balance on its slippery surface. In the distance I could see the silhouette of the columnlike rock formation that our boat had crashed into. At the base, near the water, I detected a flash of yellow. *Sophie's T-shirt!* I thought.

"That's Sophie!" I cried. "She's on the rock!" Without a moment's hesitation I dived back into the water and began swimming as fast as I could.

Sophie, just hang on with your good arm until I get there, I told her silently, my own arms slicing through the choppy surf. The waves hit me in the face, and the visibility was practically nothing. I concentrated on my stroke, and tried not to think about the shark that Mr. Conti had said he'd caught not too far away, by Gull Island.

Finally I reached the rock. Sophie was there, barely managing to cling to its mossy surface. Her red hair was plastered down on her head.

"Kayla!" She seemed very relieved to see me. "Where's everyone else?"

"On the island," I told her. "Come on."

"I can't swim in this current with my cast," she said.

"That's okay, I'll tow you," I told her.

She looked scared.

"Don't worry, Sophie," I said. "I'll get you there safely. Come on. You can't hang on to this rock forever."

She nodded and let her good arm slip down from the rock. I took hold of it, and we slowly made our way toward the island together. It was rough going, but I kept at it. *Sophie's depending on you,* I told myself. *You can't let her down.*

Finally we reached the island. Alex and Carson helped pull Sophie up onto the rock. I climbed up after her, my arms aching.

"Nice job, Kayla," Becca said. "That makes *three* rescues this month for you, you know."

"Yeah, thanks, Kayla," Sophie said in a low voice. "I guess you saved my life."

I didn't say anything. I couldn't feel happy about what I'd done. Not now. Not when I knew that *I* was the one who'd gotten everybody into this mess to begin with.

SIXTEEN

We sat together, huddled on the rock.

"So what are we going to do?" Sophie asked in a worried-sounding voice.

"The way I see it we don't have too many options," Alex replied. "We have no boat, no hope of getting a boat, and no way of letting anyone know where we are."

"You guys, I'm sorry," I said. "I know this was all my idea."

"Don't worry, Kayla," Carson said. "It's not your fault. We all wanted to come with you. You didn't force anyone to do anything."

"That's right," Becca put in. "We all wanted to do anything we could to save the island."

"And I'm sure we'll be able to flag down a passing boat in the morning," Alex added. "Meanwhile, the best thing we can probably do right now is to try to find someplace a little drier than this rock to spend the night."

"I saw some caves on this side of the island from the boat," Sophie volunteered. "Maybe we could hide out in one of them."

I nodded. "I saw them, too." I shivered. The rain had let up, but I was soaked to the skin. "Sophie, you'd better stay here, though. The rocks are slippery, and you've only got one good arm to catch yourself with. The rest of us can split up and look for a cave."

"Let's go in teams," Carson suggested. "Just to be safe." She paused. "There's no telling what might be living in these caves."

I shivered a little, thinking of the shark, octopus, and eel Mr. Conti had been catching. *Do any of those things like to hang out in island caves?* I wondered. I tried to put it out of my mind.

Becca and I set off in the direction of the northern part of the island, while Alex and Carson took the southern half. We had agreed to keep our search to the side of the island that faced the open sea, and avoid entering the sea lions' territory. Even though the animals had never threatened me in any way when I'd come to observe them, I wasn't sure how they'd feel about our being on the island itself. It was also possible that they might be extra sensitive right now because of the coming storm. In addition, the craggy, rocky landscape of the far side of the island made it a more likely place to find caves.

Becca and I picked our way over the slimy rocks, taking care as we stepped from one to the next. The rain had pretty much stopped now, but the wind seemed to go right through my wet clothes. *At least a cave will give us some shelter from the wind,* I reasoned.

I spotted a narrow opening that was about four feet tall between two rocks.

"What about that?" I asked Becca, pointing. "If there's enough room inside, it looks like it would give us pretty good shelter."

"Let's go take a look," Becca agreed.

We made our way over the rocks to the entrance of the grotto. I peered between the rocks, but all I could see was darkness. The air was cool, and there was a vaguely fishy smell.

"I sure could use a flashlight now," I said.

"While you're at it, order me some dry clothes," Becca said. "And a boat. Actually, make that a plane."

I smiled at her. "I think this should be fine for the night," I said, indicating the tunnel. "Let's go get the others."

A short while later the five of us stood in front of the entrance to the cave.

"Okay, let's check it out," Alex said, heading toward the opening between the rocks.

"Wait," Carson said, her voice filled with alarm.

I turned to look at her.

"I can't go in," she said. "It's too dark."

"I'm sure we'll be fine, Carson," Becca said reassuringly. She laughed. "Hey, if a city kid like me can brave this cave, a natural-born ranger like you shouldn't have any trouble."

Carson shook her head. "You don't understand. I need to be able to see. Without my sight I won't have any idea where I am, or what's happening." She paused.

"I won't have any way to communicate with you guys."

"Oh," I said, understanding at last. *If Carson goes into that cave, the whole world will seem silent and dark,* I realized. *She won't even be able to read our lips.* "Carson's right," I told the others. "She needs to be able to see."

"You *will* be able to see in a few minutes," Sophie assured her. "You just have to give your eyes a chance to adjust. It's all about receivers in your eyes. Alex explained it to me once."

"That's *receptors,* not *receivers,*" Alex corrected her. "Anyway, Sophie's right. Besides, you can't stay out here all night, Carson. It's cold. And it might start to rain again."

"Carson, I'll hold your hand on the way in," I promised. "We can go in together, so you won't feel so . . . cut off."

Carson pursed her lips. "Okay," she said with a quick nod. "I'll do it."

Alex led the way, with Sophie right behind her. I followed with Carson, and Becca took up the rear.

Carefully I crept along the cave wall behind Sophie. I held Carson's hand with my left hand and felt along

the wall with my right as we went. The air was cool
and smelled like seaweed.

After a few moments my eyes began to adjust to the
light, just as Sophie had predicted. I was able to make
out Alex and Sophie's silhouettes in front of me, and
the cave walls on either side.

I turned to Carson. She nodded and let go of my
hand. Then she flashed me a thumbs-up sign. I couldn't
really make out the expression on her face, but she
seemed to be doing okay.

"I see an open area up ahead," Alex called from
the front of the line. "I think there might even be some
light in there. Follow me, everybody."

A few moments later we entered a wider part of the
cave. Alex was right; there was light coming from a
small opening near the top of the cave.

I could make out everyone's faces now.

Carson's looked relieved.

Becca's looked skeptical. "Do you think this place is
rainproof?" she asked, pointing up to the hole.

Alex nodded. "Most of it is, at least. If it starts
raining, we can move over to the side, where it's more
sheltered."

Just then I heard a sound like a distant cry.

I froze.

"What was that?" Sophie asked, looking around in alarm.

I heard the sound again.

"I think it was a sea lion," I said. "But I'm not absolutely sure. I've never really heard one make that exact type of cry before." I looked up at the patch of sky. The clouds were darker now, and I realized that evening was on its way. I tried not to think about what the damp cave would be like when the sun went down and left us in darkness.

Then something in one of the cave's walls just under the skylight caught my eye. It was a hole, about two feet in diameter, and about three feet off the ground. I walked over and peered into it.

"This looks like a little tunnel," I told the others. "I wonder where it leads to."

Just then I heard another cry, louder than the others.

"Wherever it leads to, it sounds like there are sea lions there," Becca said, coming closer.

"Something about the sound of that sea lion doesn't seem right," I said. "I'm going to check this out." I hoisted myself up to the level of the hole and put my head and shoulders into the mouth of the tunnel.

The sea lion cries were loud and clear now. And it definitely seemed like the animals were in distress.

I dropped back to the floor of the cave and turned to the others. "I think there are sea lions in trouble at the other end of this tunnel," I explained. "I want to climb through and see what I can find."

"I thought you said we should stay away from the sea lions," Sophie said.

"I did," I said. "But I have a feeling this may be an emergency situation."

"I'll come with you," Alex volunteered.

"I guess you'd better count me out, Kayla," Sophie said. She held up her right arm in its damp cast.

"I'll go, Kayla," Carson said suddenly.

I looked at her. "Are you sure?"

She nodded. "I'll be okay."

"Don't all leave me alone, you guys," Sophie pleaded. "Becca, you'll stay here with me, right?"

"Sure thing, Soph," Becca replied.

I hoisted myself up to the mouth of the tunnel once more and pulled my upper body into it. It was harder to move along inside it than I had imagined, but I managed to shimmy along on my elbows and my belly, making slow but steady progress. It helped that a lot of the tunnel was angled downward, like a ramp.

I could hear Carson and Alex behind me, their bodies shuffling along through the dirt and rocks that lined the bottom of the tunnel. Ahead of me I heard an occasional sad-sounding sea lion wail.

After a couple of minutes I could also hear the rhythmic sound of water lapping against something. A strong animal smell greeted my nostrils.

Finally the end of the tunnel was in sight. I continued crawling toward it. At last I reached the end, pushing my head and shoulders out the other side. To my surprise, another face was practically nose to nose with my own. Even in the dim light I recognized who it was at once.

"Bumper!" I cried.

SEVENTEEN

I tumbled out of the mouth of the tunnel, followed by Carson and Alex. We landed together in a heap on a flat piece of rock.

I untangled myself from the others and looked around. There, to my surprise, were a half dozen sea lions perched on rocks. Bumper and King were among them. I longed to go to Bumper and stroke her sleek fur, but I knew I should probably keep my distance.

"Oh, my gosh!" Carson breathed. "Look at all of them!"

King let out a mournful bellow.

"Do you think they live here?" Alex asked nervously. "I mean, did we just invade their space or something?"

"No," I assured her. "This is definitely not their home. I recognize a couple of these animals. This is not their usual spot at all."

"Well, then, what are they doing here?" Alex asked.

"That's what I'd like to know," I replied. I looked around. We were clearly in another cave. There were several rocks like the one we were standing on, but the main part of the cave floor was submerged under water.

Just then I heard Becca's voice calling from the other side of the tunnel.

"Are you guys all right? Did you find the end?"

I stuck my head back inside the tunnel. "We're fine," I called back. "There's a bunch of sea lions down here."

I pulled my head back out of the tunnel. A couple of sea lions were watching me with interest.

"You guys, it's awfully light in here for a cave, don't you think?" Carson said suddenly.

Alex nodded. "Maybe there's another opening."

I looked up. "Not in the ceiling."

"No," Alex said. "I hear the ocean. Waves."

I listened. I could hear it, too. Plus another sound, far away, but definitely heading toward us.

"A boat!" I yelled.

Alex nodded excitedly. "I hear it, too!"

Carson's face lit up. "Is it really a boat?"

"I'll tell Becca and Sophie," I said, turning back toward the tunnel.

"Let's just go this way instead," Alex suggested. "Toward the light and the sound. I have a feeling the mouth of the cave might be just around that corner there."

"I agree with Alex," Carson said. "By the time Becca and Sophie get back out of that cave the boat may already have passed the island. Let's look for an exit this way."

"Okay, that makes sense to me," I replied. *After we get the boat's attention we can always go back for Becca and Sophie,* I reasoned.

I followed Alex and Carson away from the tunnel opening, picking my way carefully across the rocks that lined the cave wall. I noticed the sea lions watching our progress intently. King let out another painful-sounding cry, and the others joined the chorus.

I wonder what they're doing down here, I thought.

They certainly don't seem happy. But if there really is an opening to the cave up ahead, why don't they just leave and swim back around to the other side of the island?

Just then Alex stopped in her tracks. "What the—"

I stared ahead of me, shocked by what I saw. We had reached the mouth of the cave, all right. And now it was totally clear to me why none of the sea lions were leaving.

The opening was entirely blocked off by a large net!

EIGHTEEN

"What's going on?" Carson asked incredulously.

"I'll tell you what's going on," I said, my blood boiling with anger. "Someone put up this net to keep the sea lions from getting out. Someone who wants to trap them here."

"But there must be some way out," Carson said. "This is ridiculous." She leaned over the water from the rock we were standing on. She grabbed a piece of the net and tugged. But the net held firm.

"Wait a minute, I don't hear the boat anymore!" Alex exclaimed. "Quick, let's get back to the tunnel and tell Becca and Sophie to check out what's going on."

"I hope we didn't miss it," Carson said anxiously.

We scrambled over the rocks, back toward the tunnel. When we reached it, I stuck my head inside.

"Becca! Sophie!" I called. "There's a boat outside!"

"We know," Sophie called back, her voice sounding kind of funny.

"Okay, then go out and try to signal it to come to the island and help us!" I called.

"It already came to the island," Sophie replied. "And some people got off. I don't think they're going to want to help us very much, though." Her voice was filled with dread. "It's Deborah and Derek."

"Are you sure?" I asked incredulously.

"Positive," she answered. "We can hear them walking around on the rocks above us and talking."

Then we were right! Deborah and Derek are the ones who've been coming out here. And I'll bet anything they're the ones who put up that awful net.

Suddenly, as if on cue, I heard footsteps crunching in the dirt above the tunnel's ceiling. A couple of rocks came loose and tumbled down the tunnel, landing at my feet.

I turned to Carson and Alex. "Deborah and Derek are here on the island," I explained. "It was their boat."

Carson's eyes widened. "Are you positive?"

I nodded. "They're walking around right on top of us right now."

A bunch more rocks loosened and tumbled from the ceiling of the tunnel.

Alex looked concerned. "They'd better watch out, or they're going to—"

Her sentence was cut off by a sudden avalanche of falling rocks and dirt. The debris tumbled down the tunnel, spraying dust in my face. I backed up, frantically trying to brush the dirt from my eyes.

A moment later I opened them. And I couldn't believe what I saw.

The tunnel's ceiling had completely collapsed. And the entrance was blocked by a huge pile of dirt and rocks.

There was no way out!

NINETEEN

"This is awful!" I cried. "We're stuck in here!"

"You guys, I think I have even worse news," Carson said in a low voice.

"What could possibly be worse than this?" Alex asked.

"The tide," Carson replied. "It's rising." She pointed down to the rock we were standing on.

I lowered my eyes. I hadn't noticed it, but suddenly my shoes were covered with water. "Oh, my gosh, you're right!" I cried. "The tide's coming in! How high do you think the water gets in here?"

Alex put her hand on the mossy wall of the cave. "Pretty high," she responded. "There are snails and barnacles and stuff pretty much all the way up to the ceiling."

I felt my heart pounding with fear. "We have to get out of here."

"But how?" Carson asked.

"The net," I replied. "We have to rip it open."

"Let's give it a try," Alex agreed.

We all hurried back over the rocks to the mouth of the cave. I stared through the mesh for a moment at the ocean beyond, a funny feeling in my chest.

In just a little while that ocean is going to come in here and fill up this cave, I thought with dread. *We have to get out of here. And we have to let the sea lions out, too.*

Alex leaned out from the rock over the water and took hold of a piece of net. "This stuff is really tough," she said, pulling at it. "I think it's reinforced nylon. Designed not to rip," she added.

"Oh, great," I said. Then I had an idea. "Maybe we can cut it!"

"With what?" Carson asked.

I looked around. "With rock!" I bent down and picked up a flat, rough stone.

"Good idea," Alex agreed. She found a similar stone for herself and one for Carson.

We all hesitated, staring at the net, which was stretched taut over the opening of the cave, and almost unreachable from the rock we were standing on.

"Well, I guess it's time for another dip," I said, trying to sound cheerful. *This time I think I'll take off my shoes,* I added to myself.

I kicked off my soaked sneakers and jumped into the water with my cutting rock in my hand. Carson and Alex followed. We swam to the net.

"Let's work on these threads over here by the edge," Alex suggested, grabbing onto the net. "Maybe we can create an opening."

I grabbed a piece of netting and began sawing away, with Carson and Alex working right beside me. The hardest part was keeping myself afloat while I worked.

After twenty minutes of hard work we had succeeded in cutting a smallish hole in the net. My arms were sore, and the tips of my fingers were scratched and bloody.

"I think we might be able to squeeze through that!" Alex said excitedly, stretching the opening as wide as it would go.

"What about the sea lions?" I reminded her. "We can't just leave them here to drown!"

"They'll never fit through a hole this size," Carson said.

"You're right," Alex said. "Somebody has to go out and tell Becca and Sophie that we're okay, though. They must be getting worried."

"I have an idea," I said. "You guys swim out through the hole. One of you can get the message to Becca and Sophie, and one of you can try to see what Derek and Deborah are up to. I'll stay here and work on the net."

"Okay, sounds good to me," Alex said.

I watched as first Carson and then Alex squeezed her way through the hole in the net and swam away.

I turned to look at the sea lions in the cave. The tide level had risen some more, and they had all been forced off the low rocks into the water. Bumper swam back and forth, almost as if she were pacing. Her dark eyes looked big and sad.

"Don't worry," I whispered, "I'll get you guys out of here."

I went back to work on the net, rubbing at the nylon with new energy. I snapped first one cord, and then another.

Still not big enough, I said to myself. *King, for one, will definitely never make it through unless I cut at least three more cords.*

I kept at it, moving my feet underwater to try to keep myself afloat. The saltwater was stinging the cuts on my hands, and I was exhausted and cold. But I wasn't about to give up.

Finally I was finished. The hole was definitely large enough for the sea lions to make it through one at a time. *But how am I going to convince them to come through this net?* I wondered.

Bumper was still swimming back and forth anxiously.

"Bumper," I called gently. "Bumper, come on over."

She continued swimming.

I guess she has pretty good reason not to trust human beings after what Deborah and Derek tried to do to her, I thought.

"Bumper," I tried again. "Come on, Bumper. I'm going to take you back to your baby."

Bumper began to swim in wide circles, inching closer to me with each pass.

"Come on, girl, that's right, Bumper," I coaxed.

But how to get her through the net? *Maybe if she*

sees me go through she'll realize that it's a way to escape, I thought.

"Bumper, watch me," I said. I dived through the opening and swam to the other side of the net. "Come on, Bumper. You can do it."

Sure enough, Bumper changed course, heading straight for the net. She found the hole and swam out easily.

"Good job, Bumper!" I said, treading water as she swam by me.

Suddenly I heard a splash. I turned just in time to see another cow swim through the opening in the net. A few moments later a young bull followed.

I laughed. They looked like dogs at the circus, jumping through hoops.

Finally all the sea lions had come through except for King, who was still nosing the net from the other side.

"Come on, King!" I called. "I know you're not used to this kind of exercise, but you can do it. Come on!"

After a moment's hesitation, King propelled himself forward at last and came soaring through the net. He landed with a huge splash not too far from me.

I looked around me, amazed. I was surrounded by sea lions. Free sea lions. I watched happily as they headed around the corner of the island.

Then I heard the sound of a motor approaching.

Is that another boat? I thought hopefully.

A moment later a familiar sleek blue speedboat rounded the corner. *Oh, no,* I thought, panicking. *It's Deborah and Derek. I've got to hide somewhere!*

But to my surprise, it was Alex who was at the helm of the boat. And Sophie, Becca, and Carson were seated behind her.

I waved. "Over here!" I called happily.

Alex brought the boat around toward me and cut the motor.

"I'll swim out to you," I called.

But just then I heard a voice to my right. I turned and saw Deborah step out from behind a rock.

"So *that's* where our boat disappeared to!" she said angrily. "Derek! Derek, come here at once!"

"Swim!" Becca urged me from the boat. "Hurry, Kayla. We can still get away!"

I started to swim for the boat as fast as I could. A moment later I heard a splash in the water behind me, followed by another one.

"Swim faster!" Sophie called. "They're coming!"

I put every ounce of power I had into swimming. My heart was pounding like crazy. *How close are they behind me?* I wondered. *Don't look back,* I warned myself. *You'll lose valuable time.*

Finally I made it to the boat, and Carson and Becca hauled me over the edge. I collapsed on the deck, my heart still pounding crazily.

"Start the boat, Alex!" Carson cried. "They're almost here!"

I dragged myself to the side of the boat to look. Deborah was only a few feet away, and Derek was right behind her. I watched in horror as Deborah reached out and grabbed hold of the side of the boat.

"Alex!" I called. I scrambled to my feet.

The engine started, and the boat began to move. But it was too late. Deborah was already pulling herself over the side.

I heard my father's voice in my head. *Think fast. Stay on your toes. Anticipate your opponent's next move.*

Deborah had her head and shoulders over the rail now. I breathed in and delivered a smooth, swift kick directly to her left shoulder, forcing the sound out of my gut and up through my throat. *"Eeeeeow!"*

A shocked expression on her face, Deborah fell back into the water with a splash.

TWENTY

I gazed at the new sign at the park dock with pride.

> ## CAYENGA PARK
> ## SEA LION HABITAT VISITOR CENTER
>
> "SEAL ISLAND"
> BOAT DEPARTS HERE
> PLEASE PURCHASE BOAT TICKETS AT THE
> BOATHOUSE BEFORE BOARDING

"That sure looks a lot better than the Salty Dog sign would have," Becca commented.

"I'm so glad they had to take all those ugly things down," Carson agreed.

"Just think, the park's opening a visitor center on Seal Island, and the Salty Dog's out of business for good," Sophie said with satisfaction.

Becca laughed. "Is it true that Deborah and Derek's daddy took it away from them?"

"That's right," Alex said. "My father says everyone's talking about it down at the yacht club. Apparently, Mr. Randolf, their dad, is some big business tycoon. He gave Derek and Deborah the Salty Dog to run to kind of prove themselves."

"Well, they sure did prove themselves," Becca said. "They proved themselves to be class-A number-one jerks!"

"I guess Mr. Randolf was pretty upset at having to pay all those fines and stuff for them," Alex continued. "At least, that's what my dad says everyone's saying."

"They should have been given more than fines for what they did," I said firmly. "They should have had to go to jail." I shook my head. "After drowning the sea lions, Derek and Deborah were selling the bodies. That was the main ingredient in Mr. Conti's 'special bait.'" I shuddered at the thought. "We should really get the town council to make tougher laws about animal cruelty."

"Uh-oh, watch out," Becca said. "Super-Kayla's on another mission."

"Super-Kayla, huh?" said a familiar deep voice behind me.

"Dad!" I turned around. My mother and father were standing together. "Hi, Mom. Everybody, this is my mom and my dad."

My mother smiled. "Nice to meet you all." She nodded to Alex. "Good to see you, Alex." She looked around. "Well, it looks like a lovely day for a boat ride. When do we sail?"

"In just a couple of minutes, I think," I replied.

We all walked down the dock to where the new visitors' center boat was docked. A small crowd was already waiting to board.

"Tickets, please," said the ranger standing at the end of the dock.

I followed the line of visitors onto the new boat and found a spot by the rail. Just as we were about to depart, Ranger Abe came running up the dock.

"Wait! Wait!" he cried. He jogged to the boat and jumped on. Then he grinned. "I wouldn't want to miss the very first voyage."

I raised my eyebrows. "Ranger Abe, aren't you forgetting something?"

He looked concerned. "Forgetting?"

"Your ticket," I reminded him.

"Oh, that's right!" Ranger Abe cried. "I was in such a rush I forgot to buy one."

"Well, just make sure you do it when we get back," I told him. I grinned. "I made someone a promise that this boat would pay for itself in no time at all—and every penny counts."

"Don't worry, Kayla," he replied with a chuckle. "I won't try to sneak a free ride."

The boat pulled away from the dock, and I looked out at the sea. It was calm today, calm and blue. In the distance I could see Seal Island on the horizon.

As we got closer, the island took shape. Suddenly the sea lions became visible, and the crowd on the boat let out a loud sigh. I felt a shiver of happiness run down my spine.

There was Bumper, playing with her pup in the water. The pup had grown since the last time I'd seen it. And there was King, in his usual spot. Meanwhile, Jason and Sophie were battling it out over a sunny spot on a rock. Everything on Seal Island was as it should be.

Suddenly I heard a voice behind me. "I just want you to know I'm giving up."

I turned and saw Becca standing beside me.

"Giving up?" I asked her. "Giving up what?"

"Counting," she said.

I shook my head. "I don't get it. Counting what?"

"Rescues," she said. "I was keeping track for the bird and the little boy and Sophie, but when you got to all those sea lions I decided to stop counting."

I smiled. *I never thought of it that way,* I realized. *But I guess I did rescue the sea lions. I suppose my rescue instinct is still doing okay after all. Maybe I'll even get the lifeguarding shift tomorrow at the park,* I thought happily.

What was it Buddha had said? Something about disliking evil, feeling peace, and learning . . . *Well, I guess evil could be Deborah and Derek, and I certainly disliked them enough,* I thought. *And feeling peace— well, I feel pretty peaceful right now. As far as learning goes, I not only learned a whole lot, but now other people are going to be able to learn, too, by visiting the center on the island. What was the end of that quote? Oh, yeah . . . "fear will disappear." Hey, maybe that Buddha guy did know a thing or two about lifeguarding after all.*

Kayla Adams
Harmon Academy
"Communities"
Ms. Saslow

A+
Kayla: Great paper!
I loved the personal touch
of handwriting it!

An Island Community

Right here in Cayenga there is a community whose existence was, until recently, being threatened. These unique citizens of Cayenga are part of a special community, a community whose members watch out for one another, and who band together for protection from outside forces. They are also a misunderstood community—for example, many outsiders don't even know what to call them!

The community in question is a group of sea lions . . .

ALL-NEW! ALL-EXCITING! ALL GIRL-FRIENDLY!
GRAND PRIZE: $500 WORTH OF CAMPING EQUIPMENT. 50 RUNNERS-UP: GIRLS R.U.L.E. T-SHIRTS.

No purchase necessary. For complete details see below. To enter the drawing, fill in the information below and return it to:

girls
R.U.L.E.

375 Hudson Street, Dept. JH
New York, New York 10014

NAME_____

ADDRESS_____

CITY_____ STATE_____

ZIP_____ PHONE #_____

Mail this entry form or a plain 3" x 5" piece of paper postmarked no later than 12/31/98.

1. On an official entry form or a plain 3" x 5" piece of paper print or type your name, address, and telephone number and mail your entry to
GIRLS R.U.L.E. SWEEPSTAKES, THE BERKLEY PUBLISHING GROUP, DEPT. JH, 375 Hudson Street, New York, New York 10014. No purchase necessary.

2. Entries must be postmarked no later than December 31, 1998. Not responsible for lost or misdirected mail. Enter as often as you wish, but each entry must be mailed separately.

3. The winner will be determined in a random drawing on January 8, 1999. The winner will be notified by mail.

4. This drawing is open to all U.S. and Canadian (excluding Quebec) residents age 13 and over. If a resident of Canada is selected in the drawing, he or she may be required to correctly answer a skill question to claim a prize. Void where prohibited by law. Employees (and their families) of Penguin Putnam Inc., Pearson, plc and their respective affiliates, retailers, distributors, advertising, promotion and production agencies are not eligible.

5. Taxes are the sole responsibility of the prize-winner. The name and likeness of the winner may be used for promotional purposes. The winner will be required to sign and return a statement of eligibility and liability/promotional release within 14 days of notification.

6. No substitution of the prize is permitted. The prize is non-transferable.

7. In the event there is an insufficient number of entries, the sponsor reserves the right not to award the prize.

8. For the name of the prize-winner, send a self-addressed, stamped envelope to GIRLS R.U.L.E. SWEEPSTAKES, Dept. JH, The Berkley Publishing Group, 375 Hudson Street, New York, NY 10014.

9. The Berkley Publishing Group and its affiliates, successors and assigns are not responsible for any claims or injuries of contestants in connection with the contest or prizes.